SONNY AND LEO

HOLIDAY OMEGAS: VOLUME ONE

C.W. GRAY

❀ Created with Vellum

PART I
CAULDRON CAKE POPS AND A WITCH'S KISS

Holiday Omegas: Book One

CHAPTER 1

*S*onny hung over the railing of his balcony and watched the parking lot below. His newest neighbor shut the door of his truck and stretched his arms over his head, working out the kinks in his muscular back. The late evening sun cast shadows over his face, and Sonny wished he could get a glimpse of Leo's beautiful brown eyes.

Sonny yelped and gripped the rail hard when his small white cat, Flufflepuff, purred and wound around his ankles, startling him.

"You're going to fall over the rail and land on him," Aaron said, yawning. Sonny's best friend sat in a patio chair with his feet propped up. The rabbit shifter had just finished a long day of waiting tables at the diner across the street. "I swear the heels on your shoes get higher every day."

Sonny glared at his friend. "Hush it. You're interrupting my ogle time." He looked down again and whined. Leo was gone. "I only got twenty-two seconds."

Aaron rolled his eyes. "You're pathetic. Why don't you just ask the man out?"

Sonny ran a hand through his short hair. "He's way out of my league, Aaron. Plus, I don't even know if he's gay."

Aaron growled, and Sonny tried not to laugh. His friend was small with white-blond hair and large front teeth. He was probably the least-frightening person in the whole city.

Sonny thought of Aaron eating lettuce in his shifted form and couldn't hold back his laugh. "I love your growls."

"Don't laugh," Aaron said, disgruntled. "Leo isn't out of your league. If anything, you're out of his."

Sonny sat down and crossed his legs. "Have you seen all those yummy muscles? I know you saw him helping Myrtle with her groceries yesterday. He's handsome, sweet, and hardworking. How am I possibly out of his league?"

Flufflepuff jumped onto Sonny's lap, so he scratched her head before stroking her sides and back. Her butt popped into the air, and he scratched that too.

Aaron grinned. "You're going to make me say it, aren't you?"

Sonny propped his chin on his fist and gave Aaron an expectant look.

"You're an exceptional person," Aaron said, voice bored. "You're generous, kind, and creative. Oh, and your ass is really nice. There. Are you happy?"

4

"I don't feel like you really mean it," Sonny said, eyes narrowed.

Aaron sighed. "You're so needy. Do me now."

Sonny smiled wide. "You're the most talented chef in the city. You're a handsome and creative genius, who will one day own your own restaurant and be the envy of every chef in the country."

Aaron arched an eyebrow.

"Oh," Sonny said. "I forgot. You also have the ass of a Greek god. Gemma is the luckiest woman in the world."

"You two are so weird," Gemma said from the patio door. Aaron's wife leaned against the frame and watched them in amusement.

"Hey, hon," Aaron said. "We're just reaffirming each other's greatness. Best friends do that."

"He leaves footprints in my heart," Sonny said, tilting his head to the side and grinning.

Aaron cackled. "Leo leaves footprints in your–"

"Hush," Sonny hissed, but it was too late.

Gemma's eyes grew wide, and she bounced in place. "Sonny loves Leo. Sonny loves Leo."

Stupid rabbit shifters and their nosy perkiness, he thought, groaning.

"He won't do anything about it," Aaron said, making a face. "He just pines on his balcony like some angst-filled teenager."

"You're a witch," Gemma said. "Can't you just make a love potion or something?"

Aaron winced and shook his head furiously. "Been there, done that."

5

Sonny gave her a flat look. "Do you want lovesick zombies, because that's how you get lovesick zombies."

Gemma wrinkled her nose. "What the hell?"

Sonny sat back and pulled Flufflepuff close to his chest, stroking her head. "It was seventh grade. Aaron was desperately in love with Suri Harish."

Aaron smiled softly. "The prettiest girl in the school."

Gemma's eyes narrowed. "Do I need to cut a bitch?"

"Settle down, bunnies," Sonny said, waving a hand. "I'm telling a story. Anyway, Aaron was all pitiful and lovelorn."

"I was brooding in a very manly way," Aaron protested.

"Since I was his best friend and the most generous person to ever walk this earth, I decided to help him out with a love potion." Sonny puffed his chest out. "I was just Myrtle's apprentice at that point and the potion was very challenging, but I wanted to help my friend."

"He fucked it up," Aaron said, shrugging. "He put it in the punch bowl at the school dance."

Gemma covered her mouth. "Why would you do that?"

Sonny blinked. "It seemed like a good idea at the time."

"Almost every kid in the place wanted me," Aaron said, grinning before he scowled. "Then things got a little out of control."

"They *wanted* him any way they could get him," Sonny said, wincing. "They tore his clothes to pieces so they could have a strip of cloth that was close to his skin. I'm quoting here. Someone actually said that. It was disgusting."

"Then, it was my hair," Aaron said, running a hand over his head to seemingly remind himself his hair was still there. "The principal locked me in a utility closet for the rest of the night so the potion could wear off."

"They were all like, *give me the bunny*!" Sonny held out his arms and moaned.

"He got in so much trouble," Aaron said, sticking his tongue out at Sonny. "Apparently, love potions are illegal for a reason."

"I was eleven, and the potion recipe was in my advanced spell book." Sonny shuddered. "One girl attacked me for standing too close to him. They really need to leave the illegal spells *out* of the spell books."

Now, of course, Sonny understood why love potions were a bad idea. They temporarily took away a person's free will. He would never be able to live with himself if he took advantage of a person in that situation.

Gemma made a face. "Okay. So, no love potion. Maybe he could just ask him out. Leo seems nice, even if he is a bear shifter."

"His chest is so... bearlike," Sonny said, mind drifting to Leo.

"See what I have to deal with on a daily basis?" Aaron pulled Gemma onto his lap. "Like I said – pathetic."

"Have you seen his belly?" Sonny sighed and kissed

Flufflepuff's head. "It's a little soft, but in just the right way."

Gemma snickered. "I kinda think he could have a lizard tail and you'd still like him."

"Just ask the bear out," Aaron said and nibbled Gemma's shoulder.

"Why would he want to go out with me?" Sonny bit his lip. "I'm a kitchen witch working in his old mentor's potion shop. I'm too... I make people uncomfortable."

Aaron gave Sonny a sad look, and he knew his friend understood what was left unsaid. Sonny's parents had accepted him being gay since he was an omega. They *could not* handle his penchant for wearing feminine clothes and makeup. Omega or not, in their minds, he was supposed to be a man. To them, gender was a definitive thing, not complex and flexible.

Sonny just wanted to be himself without any stupid expectations. Sometimes he liked heels and skirts and pretty jewelry while other times he was fine in his jeans and t-shirts. His head knew there wasn't anything wrong with that, but sometimes he just wanted his parents to love and accept him.

"You're perfect just how you are," Aaron said grumpily. "Only an idiot wouldn't fall in love with you."

"Leo doesn't seem like an idiot," Gemma said, rubbing her chin on Aaron's shoulder. "The Halloween party is tomorrow. I've invited him to come, and you'll make your move then."

"Oh, will I?" Sonny tried to look haughty but probably just looked like he had something up his nose.

"Yes," Gemma said, giving him a hard look. "You will."

~

LATER THAT NIGHT, SONNY WORKED WITH HIS NEW apprentice, Miles. The boy was only ten, but he was smart as a fox and worked hard. Sonny had never had an apprentice before, but he tried to make things fun for Miles.

"When people think of witches, they picture scary old crones that like to toss curses at innocent bystanders," Sonny said. "Of course, there are plenty of witches that do things like that, so it's easy to understand why people might fear us."

"I don't know anyone who's cursed," Miles said, leaning on the table. His familiar, a beagle puppy, slept under his chair.

"Me neither," Sonny said, shrugging. "Myrtle says they're out there though. My point is that there's a lot of misunderstanding about what witches do. For example, Myrtle and I are kitchen witches. We use our knowledge to protect the home and nourish the body and soul."

"Mom says you're the best baker in town," Miles said, smiling proudly. "She says Myrtle makes the potions, and you bake comfort goodies."

Sonny laughed. "That's Myrtle and me alright. Then, there are garden witches, hedge witches, and a ton more. Despite seeing all of us on a daily basis, people still picture that old crone image."

Flufflepuff jumped on the table and sat on her haunches. Miles scratched her head. "Flufflepuff thinks that's stupid, don't you, girl?"

"Meow."

"She said yes." Sonny nodded, hiding his smile. "Now, the greatest gift any witch can give is comfort to those hurting. You and I are going to make some cupcakes for the nursing home down the street."

"What kind of cupcakes?" Miles gave him a curious look. This was what Sonny liked best about the boy. He never dismissed a task as too menial or boring. He just asked questions and jumped into the work.

"Well, that depends on what we really want to give," Sonny said. "Many of my friends at the nursing home deal with chronic pain, and we want to help ease them any way we can."

"I like it," Miles said, smiling.

Sonny picked up the freshly chopped peppermint. "Peppermint has healing qualities and happens to be the main ingredient in this spell." He grinned. "It also goes well with chocolate."

Miles laughed, and, together, they mixed the cupcake batter, weaving in their spells at the same time. Sonny's own brand of witchcraft was a simple and direct process, so it worked well with baking.

By the time they were finished, they had two trays of chocolate cupcakes with peppermint frosting.

Sonny handed Miles a cupcake. "Good job."

Miles attacked the cupcake, demolishing it in three bites. "So good."

Sonny laughed, then handed him a napkin before

scooping Flufflepuff up and hugging her. She was such a good familiar.

Miles wiped his face and eyed Sonny curiously. "Mom said that Nona told her that you have a crush on Leo."

Sonny blushed. "Seriously? Is nothing secret anymore?"

"Why don't you just ask him out? He's really nice."

"Adults are complicated, Miles," Sonny said, sniffing. "You wouldn't understand."

Miles scowled. "You deserve to be happy. He would be an idiot to not like you."

Sonny reached out and ruffled Miles's hair. "Just for that, I'll show you my Cauldron Cake Pop recipe. They're my absolute favorite."

CHAPTER 2

*L*eo shut the hood of the Chevy Equinox in front of him, then reached for a rag to wipe the grease off his hands. It only succeeded in moving the grease around. He loved the smell of the garage, the wide-open space, and the constant bustling around.

His family owned the auto shop, and usually the place was full of noise and laughter as he worked with his brothers and sisters. Now, it was late and everyone had already gone home. The quiet bothered him, especially since he knew he was going home to an empty apartment.

This was the last vehicle for the day, so he dropped the keys off at the front desk and cleaned up his work area.

He locked the doors behind him and activated the security system before getting in his truck. The drive to his new apartment complex was fast. It was one of the reasons he had chosen to move there. When Dillion broke up with him and kicked him out of their house, he had stayed with his parents for several months, but that had been too strange.

The apartment complex was small, with only four buildings arranged in a loose circle around a wooded park, but it was shifter friendly. More importantly, an absolutely stunning kitchen witch lived in the apartment right above him.

The day he toured the complex, he had seen Sonny and known there was something special about the witch. Then, once he moved in, he finally caught a whiff of his scent. *Mate!* His bear was ecstatic, but Leo was wary. There was no doubt in his mind that Sonny was too good for Leo.

He parked his truck and got out, stretching a bit. He was thirty-four and had worked on his feet or under a car for many of those years. Dillion's words filled his head. *I want someone younger, someone who cares about his appearance. You're an old, fat grease monkey, Leo, and I can do so much better.*

He shook himself and looked up. His witch was balanced precariously against the rails of his balcony, and Leo worried that he'd fall if he wasn't careful. Before he could say anything, Sonny looked over his shoulder.

"Get a grip," he said under his breath. "No way will a beautiful witch want an old, fat bear."

"You talking to yourself?" Myrtle stood in front of his truck.

Leo blushed. "Hey. Did you need help with something?" The witch was in her sixties and completely self-sufficient, but somehow, Leo always ended up taking out her garbage.

Myrtle watched him for a moment, and he shifted from foot to foot. "I made you dinner."

Leo's stomach growled, and he grinned. "Really?"

"Come on, bear." She led him to the door of her ground-floor apartment. "Why did your parents name you Leo? You're a bear. Wouldn't Yogi or Baloo have been better?"

He snorted. "It's Leopold."

She made a face. "Okay. Cat-bear is much better than Leopold."

"I'm not a –"

Myrtle ignored him and opened her door. "I made beef stroganoff. Hope you like it."

It was no secret that she owned the apartment complex, but most wouldn't know it by her home. It was small, only a one bedroom, and cluttered to the point of messiness. Drying herbs hung in all the windows and books, trinkets, and potion bottles were piled everywhere.

Her familiar, a ferret named Toddlebug, slept on a worn-out cat stand in front of the largest window.

The table was already set, and Myrtle waved him to the sink. "Wash your hands and park your ass. I'll get you a beer."

Leo sat and sniffed the air. The woman could cook, and his belly was thankful she didn't mind sitting across from him.

Myrtle set a beer in front of him and sat down.

"Sonny is a good one, cat-bear. I don't understand why you're dragging your feet about mating him."

Leo's mouth dropped open. "How did you know?" Myrtle and he had talked about Sonny before. She told him stories from Sonny's childhood and had answered his questions about Sonny's preferred pronouns. He hadn't thought he had given himself away, but he must have.

Myrtle rolled her eyes and filled her plate. "Do I look like an idiot to you? Now, is it that nasty Dillion that's holding you back? I know a couple of curses I could use. Do you want me to curse him with flamingo feet? Oh, you should let me turn his willy into a snake. That's my favorite."

Leo gave her a suspicious look. Witches didn't read minds, did they? "How do you know about Dillion?"

"I went to your garage and met Coleen."

"Of course you did." Leo groaned and rubbed his face.

"Your sister sure is chatty. She told me all about the asshole." Myrtle narrowed her eyes. "Sonny ain't like that. He's not some hoity-toity accountant that thinks he needs a fancy businessman boyfriend. He knows what's really important."

"Uh, okay." Leo's face was on fire.

"Look. I like you, so I'm gonna help you out. You're going to Gemma and Aaron's Halloween party, right?"

"I don't know. I'm not much for parties." Leo shrugged and took a bite.

"You're going to this one, and I'll pick out your costume. It's important, cat-bear."

15

"I'm not a cat-bear." Leo didn't know why he even protested. Myrtle didn't seem the type to listen to anyone.

"You'll be a good mate," Myrtle said, then narrowed her eyes. "If you aren't, I will *definitely* turn your willy into a snake. Sonny is like a son to me." She started cackling. "Sonny. Son. See what I did there?"

~

LATER THAT NIGHT, LEO AMBLED THROUGH THE SMALL wooded park in his bear form. The sun was setting, and there were a few joggers and about a dozen shifters in the area. Right on time, Miles and his puppy, Cookie, met him on the path leading between the apartment buildings.

"Hey, Leo." Miles made sure his backpack was firmly strapped on, then gripped a handful of Leo's fur before pulling himself onto Leo's back. "Today at school, Joey and I started making our own language. We're going to call it the Moey Code. It was either that or the Jiles Code, and we think Moey sounds more sophisticated."

Laughter rumbled in Leo's chest, and he started down the path. Cookie barked and romped beside him, tongue hanging from his mouth as he ran to sniff every flower and tree they came across.

"Tonight with Sonny, I learned two recipes and three spells. I'm going to make Cauldron Cake Pops for the party tomorrow night, and you have to promise to eat all of them, okay? Promise?"

Leo grunted his agreement.

"It's really important, Leo." Miles patted his back. "Sonny is my favorite mentor. He doesn't get all snotty if I ask questions, and he has a way of making hard stuff easier. My last mentor had three apprentices, and he made us compete all the time. I hated it. I just wanted to learn, but the other two liked to play tricks and sabotage spells. I was doing a simple fire spell to get water to boil, but they messed it up and almost caught Cookie on fire. I couldn't take it anymore, and Mom made the Witches Council give me a new mentor."

Leo growled a bit. His bear suddenly liked the idea of mauling a jackass mentor.

Miles chatted as they slowly made their way to the apartment building on the other side of the park. People smiled and waved as they passed, not thinking a thing about a boy riding a large brown bear through a park.

When they arrived, Miles slid off Leo's back. "See you tomorrow, Leo. Remember, all the cake pops are for you, okay?"

Leo waited until Miles and Cookie went inside, then headed back through the woods. This had become his normal routine since he had moved in. He liked that his bear got a little exercise. His parents and siblings lived in the suburbs and had a large park behind their neighborhood, so his mom had insisted that if he was to live in the city, he pick a place with some space.

The townhouse he had shared with Dillion had been miles away from a park.

He stopped suddenly when two rabbits appeared in front of him on the path. *This isn't part of the routine.*

The male rabbit stood on his hind legs and glared at Leo. *What the hell did I do to you, bunny?* Sometimes Leo wished shifters could speak when they were shifted.

The female rabbit bumped the male aside and wiggled her nose at Leo before prodding the male to move toward the woods.

Weird, he thought and finished his walk home. Once he had shifted and quickly dressed, he went upstairs.

Just as he had feared, his apartment was empty and quiet. The floor plan was nice and open, with two bedrooms and a bathroom. The problem was that it was so bare and plain. It wasn't a home, and he desperately wanted it to be.

His home with Dillion hadn't been perfect, but Leo had been content there. He had thought they were building something together. Leo sighed and pushed those memories away. He didn't miss Dillion at all, but he did miss being with someone and planning for a future.

He showered, dressed in a pair of loose cotton pants, then grabbed a beer from the fridge.

He settled into a chair on his balcony and looked out at the stars. Leo took a deep breath and savored the tantalizing scent of his mate. Sonny smelled like Leo's favorite treat, honey cakes.

The sound of claws on wood came from his right,

and a few minutes later, Flufflepuff climbed over the rail of the balcony.

"Are you trying to scare your witch, Fluff? He'll worry about you climbing balconies."

"Meow." The cat hopped in his lap and settled in for her nightly pampering.

Leo scratched her ears and stroked her back and sides. "How's your witch doing? Did he work too hard today? He keeps long hours most of the time, doesn't he?"

According to Miles's mom, Trish, it appeared that Sonny was mostly managing the shop since Myrtle was spending less and less time there.

"You made sure he ate, right, Fluff?"

"Meow."

"Good girl." Leo scratched her head. "Myrtle called me a cat-bear today. Wasn't that rude?"

"Meow."

"You're right. What does she know anyway?"

CHAPTER 3

"*A*lright, Mr. Jones. Here are your gingersnaps and your tincture. I added a slice of the blackberry lemon pound cake I made this morning."

"That will help my arthritis?" Mr. Jones asked, eyes hopeful.

Sonny nodded. *It will also help ease your grief,* he thought. The elderly man's wife had passed away a month ago, and Mr. Jones had been a mess. The two had been married for over thirty years.

"Oh, we can't forget your Samhain candle." Sonny added it into his bag.

All Hallows Eve was a special night for spirits. With the changing of the seasons, the spirit world was much closer to their own. The candle was meant to welcome the good spirits and ward away the bad ones.

He packed up the candle, snacks, and tincture while Mr. Jones relaxed in one of the well-padded old chairs near the front window of the shop. Sonny loved Myrtle's place. Several shelves displayed potions and tinctures made by Myrtle herself while others held soaps, candles, and other usable items made by Sonny.

Then there was the dessert case. Myrtle let him have free rein with it, and he enjoyed filling it with delicious goodies spelled to soothe and ease anxiety, depression, and pain. Those were his specialty, but he also made items to boost energy and confidence.

"You're a sweetheart, Sonny." Mr. Jones pushed himself out of the chair and came to get his items. "Myrtle is lucky to have you."

Sonny grinned and gestured down his body. Today he was dressed in a frilly black skirt, loose purple blouse, and a black corset. "I *am* absolutely magnificent, aren't I?"

Mr. Jones chuckled. "You're gorgeous." He grabbed his items and pet Flufflepuff before leaving the shop.

Sonny watched him walk down the street, heart heavy. "Flufflepuff, I know losing his wife hurt him, but I want something like they had. I want my forever person."

"Meow." Flufflepuff sat in the large cat stand in the corner and licked her paws.

"You are no help." Sonny locked the door to the shop and flipped the sign to closed. Today had been exhausting. All Hallows Eve always was. They had sold out of almost everything, and Sonny was happy the store was closed tomorrow. He would need a full day to restock.

"Flufflepuff, it's costume time. Well, you've been wearing your costume all day, so really, it's costume time for me." His familiar wore a witch's hat and a

Harry Potter Hufflepuff house scarf. "I think you should wear this every day."

He looked up when someone banged on the door. Gemma waved her arms at him until he opened up.

"Hurry up, Sonny. We need to get you ready for the party." Gemma bounced in place. "Aaron finished the food and is setting things up now."

Sonny groaned. "I'm so tired, Gemma. Can I just stay home this year?"

"Absolutely not!"

Sonny grabbed his backpack and put Flufflepuff on her leash. "I don't know what the big deal is. You know I'm not going to ask Leo out. It'll be like every other time. I'll see him and suddenly develop shyness and hide behind Aaron." He snapped his fingers and the lit candles around the room went out.

"Tonight will be different," Gemma said, walking with him to the apartment complex. "Myrtle and I have a plan."

"Fuck fuckity fuck poo."

Gemma stifled a giggle. "It's not that bad."

Sonny glared at her. "I don't believe you."

"You get to wear a blond wig and a cute dress."

Sonny pursed his lips and weighed his options. "Okay. I'm in."

They walked the short distance to the apartment complex, and Gemma took him to her and Aaron's apartment. He had been there a million times, but something was different. There were more pillows and blankets on the furniture and even a little nest in the corner of the living room.

"Gemma, are you... are you nesting?"

His friend bit her lip to hide her smile. "Aaron wants to be the one to tell you, so pretend you didn't notice anything. Okay?"

Sonny whooped and picked her up, swinging her around the room. "I'm gonna be an uncle!"

"Gemma," Aaron whined from the bedroom door. "I wanted to tell him."

"He noticed my nests," she said, giggling when Sonny finally put her down.

"We're having a baby," Sonny said, picking Aaron up and spinning him too. "We should name them Chuck Norris and get them ten puppies."

"We are not naming the baby Chuck Norris," Gemma said, rolling her eyes. "What would they even do with ten puppies?"

"Obviously they would be Chuck's personal dog gang," Aaron said. "I can just see it now. Our baby rabbit running through the woods with their pack of guard dogs. I love it."

"You two are ridiculous." Gemma grabbed a pillow and smacked Sonny over the head. "Come on, Goldilocks. We need to get you ready for the party."

SONNY TUGGED ON THE HEM OF THE SHORT, YELLOW ruffled dress he wore. It was a lot shorter than the skirts he usually wore, but Gemma had insisted. "Why am I dressed like Goldilocks?"

Gemma batted her eyes and gave him an innocent

smile. "Do I really need to spell it out for you? Maybe I should get the hand puppets. Do you like your wig?"

Sonny spun back to the mirror and preened. The costume came with a wig of silky blond curls. His own short brown hair just wouldn't do tonight. "It's perfect."

Gemma was dressed in a sexy police costume. Sonny suspected real police officers didn't wear short black dresses with thigh-high boots.

"Where's Aaron?"

"At the party. Myrtle and he just finished putting out all the food." She tucked a little pack of lube and a condom in the wide white belt around his waist. "Just in case."

He arched a brow. "Seriously? I'm going to hook up with someone at a community Halloween party?"

"You never know, Sonny." Gemma patted his wig one more time, then handed him Flufflepuff. "Let's go make an entrance."

His white baby-doll heels clicked on the floor as they walked downstairs. "I'm keeping these shoes."

"Of course, you are," Gemma said dryly.

The party was set up in the community center on the bottom floor of Sonny's building. The room was already packed with the apartment complex residents and their families and friends. The children would be back from trick or treating in about an hour, so the adults were enjoying the beer while they could.

Aaron had done a good job with the decorations. Spider webs, bats, and dark fairy lights hung from the ceiling, and a fog machine created a rolling, soft white fog across the floor. Samhain candles dotted the room, all lit.

Sonny stopped in his tracks and swallowed hard. Leo stood with Myrtle. The handsome man was dressed as a bear. The furred shirt he wore left his arms bare, and fortunately he wore jeans instead of furry legs.

"Sexy bear," he whispered and made grabby hands.

"Dear lord, you have it bad," Gemma said, snickering. "He's wearing a fur hood. There's nothing sexy about that."

Myrtle saw them then and tugged Leo toward them.

"Meep!" Sonny darted behind Gemma and did his best to hide behind the smaller woman.

His mentor smiled widely. "Sonny, can you take Leo to the buffet table? I made a special treat for you."

Sonny mumbled under his breath, and Gemma laughed.

"What was that?" Myrtle glared at him.

"I said, yes, ma'am," Sonny answered.

Myrtle gave him a knowing look. "That's what I thought. You two go on. I'll bring your treats."

Sonny smiled, hoping he didn't look like a nervous maniac. "Hi, Leo."

Leo smiled shyly. "Hey."

"You two need to move before I whomp you," Myrtle said. "Go, go, go, go."

Leo bent an arm and held it out to Sonny.

I love you and want to have your babies, Sonny thought and laughed nervously before taking the bear's arm.

"The buffet table is this way, I think," Leo said and

grinned at him. "I put some Cauldron Cake Pops with the other desserts. Miles made them for me, so don't tell him, alright? I was supposed to eat them all, but I can't eat green frosting. It makes me want to puke. They were cute though."

Sonny bit his lip. "You know Miles?"

"Yeah, we're friends."

Sonny grinned. "Really? You're friends with a ten-year-old?"

Leo laughed, and Sonny wanted to laugh with him. Damn, but the bear was gorgeous when he smiled. He was gorgeous no matter what.

"He adopted me when I first moved here. His parents are nice too," Leo said, then stopped walking and winced. "Oh, shit."

"What's wrong?" Sonny glared and looked around. Nothing would upset his boo. Nothing!

Leo gave him a sad look. "My ex-boyfriend Dillion is here. That's him with Justin from 4C."

Sonny looked the skank over. The omega wasn't a witch, but Sonny didn't have a shifter nose to tell him the species of everyone he could scent. "What kind of shifter is he?"

"He's a bear shifter like me," Leo said, giving Sonny a curious look.

Leo's ex had an average build and beautiful golden blond hair. *Fucker*.

"He dressed as a sexy priest," Sonny said, snorting. "Priests aren't sexy. They don't wear tight black shorts and a sleeveless mesh shirt. It's historically inaccurate and sets a bad example."

Leo chuckled. "Historically inaccurate?"

"Leo?" Dillion frowned, looking confused. "Please tell me you're not stalking me. We're over. I told you that months ago."

Justin looked between them nervously.

Sonny's smile probably looked as fake as it felt. "Dillion, is it?"

Dillion nodded. "Yeah?"

"My honey bear lives here, so the better question is are *you* stalking Leo?" Sonny stepped closer to the man. "Fair warning, I can turn your head into a pecan pie. Just saying."

Dillion backed up. "Uh, I'm here with Justin. There's no way I'd want the tubby bear back, okay?"

Sonny narrowed his eyes and growled. "Cute words don't hide your meanness, asshole."

Myrtle's voice interrupted him from possibly becoming one of the curse-throwing crones he had told Miles about. "Sonny? I have your treat over here."

Leo steered him away from Dillion, but Sonny watched the fucker over his shoulder. "His head would be more attractive as a pecan pie."

Leo grinned, then started laughing. "Sonny, you are absolutely perfect."

Sonny's glare disappeared, and he looked back at Leo. *Goddess, I hope I don't look as besotted as I feel.*

"Sonny?" Myrtle snapped her fingers in front of his face. "You look like an adoring puppy. Snap out of it. Cat-bear knows you like him already."

Sonny held Flufflepuff up and hissed at his mentor. "Fluffepuff, attack!"

"Meow."

Sonny kissed his familiar's head. "You have shamed your family."

Leo laughed and took Flufflepuff from Sonny. "Don't you listen to your witch. You're the best familiar around."

Myrtle gave Sonny a fond look and handed him a plate with seven Cauldron Cake Pops. "These are for you, Sonny. I know they're your favorite so enjoy them. Oh yeah, you can't share them with anyone, okay? Just eat them up and leave the plate in the kitchen."

"Uh, okay?" Sonny looked at the cake pops suspiciously. "Did you make pot cake pops?"

Myrtle scowled at him. "Just eat them, Sonny, and don't share them. I saw you devour half a pound cake last week. I know you have it in you to eat seven cake pops."

Aaron ran over. "Myrtle, we're almost out of beer. Will you go with me to get more? Roger always gives you a discount."

Myrtle patted her hair. "That's because Roger knows how to treat a woman."

Sonny wrinkled his nose. He did not want to think about Myrtle and Roger getting it on.

As soon as she was gone, Sonny set the cake pops on the buffet table.

"She said not to share those," Leo said, waving to the plate. Flufflepuff crawled up Leo's chest and stretched out on his shoulder.

Sonny shrugged. "Myrtle is sweet, but she can't

bake for shit. I'm not eating her cake pops. Don't tell her though, okay? I don't want to hurt her feelings."

Leo smiled and nodded. "Sure." A slow song came over the speakers. "Do you want to dance?"

Sonny sighed happily. "This Goldilocks *really* wants to dance with his bear."

CHAPTER 4

*L*eo barely managed to not shudder in pleasure when Sonny laid his head against Leo's chest as they slowly swayed on the dancefloor. His mate was sweet and funny, and there were so many things he wanted to ask him, things he wanted to tell him.

With his mate in his arms, it suddenly didn't feel like Sonny was out of his league. Even with Flufflepuff spread out on his shoulders, this moment felt perfect. Maybe, when the dance was over, he could ask Sonny out to dinner.

"You're a good dancer," Sonny mumbled into Leo's chest.

Leo chuckled. "This kind of dancing is easy. Trust me, you don't want to see me try anything fancier."

Sonny looked up, meeting his eyes. "Why did you date Dillion? He's horrible."

"He's not horrible," Leo said. "He's just self-involved and petty."

Sonny wrinkled his nose, looking even more adorable. "I should have gone all Maleficent on his ass."

Leo settled his chin on top of Sonny's head. "Dillion's words hurt, but not as much as they used to. We lived together for a year, but I didn't realize how critical he was until we broke up. Every day was filled with little comments about my weight, the auto shop, or my family. He didn't like any of it."

Sonny growled, and Leo started laughing. He knew Sonny was a powerful witch, but he was so damn cute it was hard to take his growl seriously.

Sonny pouted. "His head really would make a nice pecan pie. The spell would only last for an hour."

Leo stroked Sonny's back, trying to soothe him. "There's no point to it now. Dillion can't hurt me anymore."

"I like your belly," Sonny mumbled, rubbing his face against Leo's chest and reminding Leo of Flufflepuff.

Leo flushed. "I'm glad. I don't think it's going anywhere."

"Being a mechanic is a good career," Sonny added. "Myrtle says your family's auto shop does good work."

"We do," Leo said, smiling softly. "My mom and my sister Coleen run the office while the rest of us handle the jobs."

"Why didn't Dillion like your family? Are they mean?"

Leo snorted, thinking about his mom and her need to feed everyone. "No. They're loud and obnoxious. They like to play jokes on one another, and we're always teasing each other. I have two sisters and three brothers. It gets a bit chaotic."

"That sounds nice," Sonny said. Leo didn't know what to make of the wistfulness in the witch's voice.

"Dillion thought they were too rough and common – his words, not mine."

"Dillion is stupid."

"Agreed." Leo closed his eyes and enjoyed the moment.

"Look at that ass," someone whispered behind him, and a small hand squeezed his butt.

"What the fuck?" Leo spun around, glaring at the woman dressed as Little Red Riding Hood.

She bit her lip and gave him a heated look. "Do you want to be my Big Bad Wolf?"

"Carrie, back off," a young man dressed like a firefighter said. "He's a bear. Obviously, he doesn't want to be your wolf." The man blew him a kiss. "Hey, bear. Do you want to see my hose?"

Leo gave Sonny a puzzled look. "Are they for real?"

Sonny narrowed his eyes and studied the two. "I think we have a problem, Leo."

"Leo, I need you," Dillion said, pushing between the other two and pressing against Leo. "Fuck me hard. Right here."

Less than a minute later, Dillion's head resembled a pecan pie, and a crowd was gathering.

"Sonny," Gemma screeched, pushing around the other partiers. "What did you do?"

"It's only an illusion spell," Sonny mumbled, and Leo laughed, earning a glare from Gemma.

"Leo is such a sexy name," another man said, this one dressed like a vampire Zorro. Oops, he *was* a vampire dressed like Zorro.

"I think they're spelled," Sonny said, wincing.

"Sonny, that dress shows off your legs so well," an elderly woman dressed as a medieval queen said. "Why don't you lift it up just a little, and let us see what's underneath."

"Mrs. Cortez," Gemma said, gasping. "Your husband is right beside you."

"I think Rosie has a good idea there," Mr. Cortez said, eyes full of lust as he looked Sonny up and down.

A deep growl rumbled through Leo's chest. *Fuckers better back off.*

Dillion, pecan pie head and all, tried to press against Leo again, but the firefighter and Little Red were vying for his spot.

"I've never noticed how pretty your eyes are, Sonny," a woman dressed as a zombie said. "Do you want to go out sometime? How about now?"

"Definitely spelled," Sonny said, eyes worried. "Gemma, this is my seventh-grade school dance all over again."

"Your dewy body glistens in the light," Zombie lady said, eyes devouring Sonny. "Let's make love all through the night. I'll wrap you in my arms so tight, and hug you with all my might."

"Wow," Leo said. "I'm both frightened and impressed."

Sonny stifled a laugh. "Damn it, this is bad."

Six more people pressed through the crowds to get

closer to Leo and Sonny, while Gemma tried to push them back.

Leo held Sonny tight and batted away the Cortezes' hands as they reached for Sonny. "What the fuck is going on?"

"Uh, I'm sorry about this, Leo," Sonny said. "I have a feeling Myrtle did something to the cake pops."

"Sonny! I need you."

"Leo! Let me touch your hair."

"I'll die if I can't have you."

"Just take the dress off. Let me see that hiney!"

"Yeah," Leo said, drawing out the word. "I think that's a good possibility."

"Sonny isn't the sexy one," the firefighter said. "The bear makes my dick so hard."

Mrs. Cortez smacked the man. "Don't you dare insult my Sonny sunshine-naked booty-shaker. He's the hottest thing in this room."

"You tell him, Rosie. Here, I'll get Sonny and bring him back to our apartment." Mr. Cortez tried to get past Gemma, but the rabbit stomped on his foot and bit his arm. "Damn, crazy rabbit!"

Trish and her husband, Raul, pushed through and started helping Gemma keep the lust-filled people away from Leo and Sonny.

"Gemma, get them somewhere safe," Trish said, whacking Zorro with her large bag and umbrella. Fortunately, Miles's mom had dressed as Mary Poppins for the party.

Leo yelped when he felt a hand pull off the furry

hood he wore, baring his dark hair. Flufflepuff hissed and swatted at Little Red.

"Gemma, we'll help too," another man in the crowd said and stepped in to fend off Little Red's grasping hands. "Back off, lady."

"Thanks, Doug. I'll get them out of here." Gemma grabbed Leo and Sonny and ran with them to the bathroom across from the manager's office. "You two stay there until Myrtle gets back. Lock the door and ignore anything you hear."

Leo looked over her shoulder. Fourteen lust-filled people were pushing the other partygoers aside and trying to get to Leo and Sonny. "Gemma."

She looked back and rolled her eyes. "You seriously owe me for this, Sonny. I can't believe I have to clean up this mess."

She pushed them into the bathroom and slammed the door.

Sonny locked the door and pushed the small accent table in front of it. He turned around and gave Leo a sad look. "Well, this is a nice first date."

Leo blinked, then grinned, his worry over the strange night disappearing. "This is a date?"

Sonny blushed. "We're wearing a couple's costume. That means it has to be a date, right?"

It didn't, but Leo wasn't about to point that out. "Yeah. It must be."

CHAPTER 5

"At least the bathroom isn't tiny," Sonny said, sitting on the small ornate chair next to the sink. The bathroom was meant for prospective renters, so Myrtle's manager kept it well decorated and in perfect condition.

Leo sat on the toilet seat. "It could be worse."

"I can't believe Myrtle made love-potion cake pops." Sonny made a face. "She should know better." He didn't understand how she had managed to direct the potion toward both Sonny and Leo.

Leo looked thoughtful. "There were only seven cake pops, but I counted fourteen people."

Sonny blinked. "Oh. That's right."

Leo sighed and leaned his head back on his shoulders, dislodging Flufflepuff. "Miles made me exactly seven cake pops too. He kept telling me to make sure to eat them all."

Sonny groaned. "What do you want to bet that he spelled the cake pops to make you fall for me, and

Myrtle spelled her cake pops to make me fall for you?"

"I think you're right." Leo frowned. "I feel bad for those people."

"Me too. It's not right to mess with people's emotions," Sonny said, feeling guilty. "At least not without their knowledge. I've made baked goods spelled with love enhancements for clients before, but it's always been with their knowledge and consent. They wanted to spice up date night."

"To be fair, Miles probably knows how much I like you," Leo said.

Sonny tapped his shoes on the tiled floor in excitement. "You like me?"

Leo smiled, and Sonny's heart thumped faster. His bear was a handsome man. "I like you way too much."

"It could never be too much," Sonny said, shaking his head. "Myrtle knows I have a teeny tiny crush on you too. She probably thought she was just giving me a little push."

"A teeny tiny crush?"

Sonny held his fingers up, an inch of space between his thumb and index finger. "Teeny tiny."

Leo scratched his chin. "Now that I think about it, you're always watching me from your balcony when I get home from work."

Sonny smiled. "Okay. It may be a huge, gigantic, colossal crush."

Leo's smile lit up his face. "Why didn't you say anything before? We've been dodging one another for a few months now."

Sonny stretched his legs out and gestured over his outfit. "I wasn't sure how you felt about all this."

"Hmm, I think all that is damn beautiful." Leo moved to sit on the floor beside Sonny's chair. "You're a beautiful person, Sonny. I've watched you too, you know. I see you with Miles and with Aaron and Gemma. Flufflepuff comes and visits me every night to tell me how wonderful you are."

The cat climbed onto Sonny's lap and purred. Sonny stroked her back. "Good kitty. Wait. How is she visiting you?"

Leo winced. "That's not important. The point is, you're a lovely person inside and out, and I'm glad you are at least somewhat attracted to me."

Sonny took a breath. "My parents weren't so happy with my genderfluidity."

Leo looked confused. "Why not? It's not a big deal. It's just you being who you are."

Sonny couldn't resist reaching out and cupping Leo's face. The bear's skin felt warm and a little rough from his evening stubble. "They aren't as understanding as you. When I was a kid, I had to hide my more feminine clothes and makeup. I kept things at Myrtle's shop, and Aaron had a drawer of clothes for me at his house. When I was feeling more feminine, I would change outfits before school. Of course, my parents caught me a time or two."

"What did they do?" Leo's voice was gruff and his eyes more golden than they should be.

His bear must be close to the surface. Sonny shrugged. "Confiscated my makeup and searched my closet for anything too girly. When I graduated high school, Myrtle and Aaron helped me move here. Myrtle gave me a job and signed over ownership of my apartment."

"What did your parents say about that?"

Sonny grinned. "They were pissed, but there's nothing they can do. I haven't spoken to them since I moved out. I call once a month and leave a message, but that's it. They never call back."

Leo covered Sonny's hand with his own. "Do you want me to kill them? I have a couple of lion shifter friends with questionable eating habits."

Sonny made a face. "Eww. No, thanks."

He held Flufflepuff carefully and leaned forward, *accidently* falling into Leo's lap. "Oops. I'm so sorry." He wiggled around until he got comfortable. "So, tell me about your family."

"Bunch of bear shifters that live in the suburbs," Leo said, shrugging. He wrapped his arms around Sonny. "My grandparents live farther north and thought my parents were crazy for moving right outside the city, but my dad wanted to start his own business, and you kinda need customers for that to work."

"Do you still talk to your grandparents?" Sonny's own grandparents were fully supportive of his parents cutting him out of their life, so the concept of a loving family was kind of odd to him.

"Oh yeah. We kids spent our summers with them when we were young. Now, we may be grown up, but we still like to visit. Usually we'll do a big holiday weekend with them in December."

Sonny grinned. "I can just see you shoveling cows and mucking cornfields. Farmer bears are so hot."

Leo laughed, and Sonny enjoyed the rumbles. "I take it you've never been to the country?"

"Nope."

Leo gave him a shy look. "If you want, you could come with us this year."

Sonny swallowed hard. "Really? Your family wouldn't mind?"

Leo shook his head and licked his lips. "No.

Sonny's eyes traced Leo's lips, and he couldn't resist. He leaned forward and pressed his mouth to Leo's. His bear tasted like heated honey, and Sonny couldn't get enough of him.

Sonny groaned and deepened the kiss, Leo's arms tightening around him. He vaguely felt Flufflepuff scamper off his lap when he moved to straddle Leo, his tongue sliding against his bear's.

Leo's warm hands ran up the sides of Sonny's bare thighs, and Sonny shuddered, dick hardening quickly. He moved his hips against Leo, feeling the shifter's erection pressing against his ass.

"Sonny," Leo said, breaking the kiss. "I can't just kiss you."

Sonny grabbed his face and pulled him in for another kiss. "Good."

Leo growled and cupped Sonny's ass as he arched up. His big hands gripped the back of Sonny's manties and pulled hard, ripping the fabric in half and baring his ass to the cool air.

"Leo," Sonny said, laughing against Leo's lips. "I would have taken them off."

Leo rubbed a finger against Sonny's hole, but he stopped laughing to moan. "Fuck. We don't have any lube."

Sonny started laughing. "I love Gemma."

Leo scowled. "Say what?"

Sonny pulled the single pack of lube and condom from his belt. "Gemma gave this to me earlier tonight, *just in case*."

Leo hummed. "I love Gemma too."

A few minutes later, Sonny gasped when Leo's finger stretched his hole. He pushed back, moaning when Leo added a second finger. "Leo, get in me. Now!"

"Bossy," Leo said, smiling against Sonny's neck.

Sonny unbuttoned Leo's pants and licked his lips at the size of his dick. He squeezed the last of the lube into his palm and slowly stroked Leo, learning the shape and the feel of his man. "I'll be spending a lot of time with you, little Leo."

Leo laughed through his moans. "Did you just talk to my dick?"

"Shh, I'm having a conversation here."

Sonny squeaked when Leo rolled him onto the soft rug and braced himself above him. "Sorry to interrupt."

Leo slowly pushed into him, and Sonny lost all ability to speak. Long, smooth strokes in and out of his ass took up all his attention until Leo leaned down and kissed him again.

I love him. I love Leo, Sonny thought, losing himself to the feel of their bodies moving together. Leo hit just the right spot and Sonny lost it, calling out and coming hard.

A few moments later, Leo came, filling Sonny's ass.

They lay together on the hard floor, panting while they caught their breath. Sonny looked to his left. Flufflepuff stared at them, eyes bored. Sonny's wig was crumpled next to her.

"Oh, goddess, what have we done?"

Leo started laughing. "I'd say we traumatized her, but she doesn't look all that scandalized."

Sonny smiled, then bit his lip. "Leo, I really want to do that again."

Leo smiled wide. "Me too."

CHAPTER 6

*L*eo woke up quickly, feeling eyes watching him. They lay on the bathroom floor, and Sonny slept sprawled on top of him.

Myrtle and Gemma looked down at them, identical smug looks on their faces.

"I told you the costumes would work," Gemma said, crossing her arms.

Myrtle snorted, and Toddlebug chittered from her shoulder. "Costumes? My cake pops brought them together."

Gemma narrowed her eyes. "No, your cake pops got you reprimanded by the Witches Council and fined by the police."

"Did Miles get in trouble?" Leo really hoped the kid didn't lose his apprenticeship with Sonny.

Gemma looked puzzled. "Why would he be in trouble?"

Myrtle shook her head furiously. "You didn't hear that, Gemma. Sweet Miles didn't have anything to do with it. I made two sets of cake pops and then didn't stick around to make sure they went to the right people. It was irresponsible, and I'll deal with it."

Leo grinned, happy that the older witch was protecting Sonny's apprentice.

Gemma sighed, then chuckled. "Miles is a lucky boy. You'll talk with him, Myrtle?"

The older witch pursed her lips. "Of course. Had to have the same conversation with Sonny when he was about Miles's age." She winced. "Got my own lecture last night. I'll take him with me when I do my round of apologies."

"Last night?" Leo yawned. "How long have we been in here?" His back was telling him he had been on the hard floor for years.

Gemma hid a smile. "I may have *forgotten* to let you two out last night. The cake pops wore off an hour after they were eaten."

Leo grinned. "I can't complain."

Sonny's head lifted from his shoulder, and he blinked groggily. "Huh? What's going on?"

Gemma snorted. "You caught your bear, Goldilocks. Get your ass up."

Sonny buried his face against Leo's neck and hugged him. "Fuck off. He's mine, and I'm never letting him go."

Gemma laughed. "Not even to get up?"

"Never!"

Leo's stomach growled. "Want to get breakfast?"

Sonny rolled off him and jumped to his feet before

helping Leo stand. His witch kept a firm grip on Leo's hand even while putting his shoes back on.

As if I'll go anywhere, Leo thought, smiling softly.

Flufflepuff jumped and climbed her way to Leo's shoulder, stretching out and settling down, long tail trailing down his back.

Sonny waved a hand at the women in the doorway. "My honey bear is hungry. Move it, you two. I need to make him some cinnamon rolls."

Gemma grinned and stooped to grab Sonny's tangled wig from the floor. "We don't even get a thank you?"

Sonny narrowed his eyes. "Thank you for arranging the couple's costume, but Myrtle, you and Miles are getting an earful once I finish feeding my man."

Myrtle turned on her heel and hustled toward the stairs, mumbling under her breath. Leo's shifter ears heard every word though. "Don't want another fucking lecture. Cat-bear needs to control his mate."

Gemma shook her head. "You turned a man's head into a pecan pie, Sonny."

"Damn it, it was just an illusion," Sonny said, glaring at Gemma. "The fucker touched my bear."

Leo felt giddiness bubble through him. His mate liked him. Sonny wanted him so much he was willing to fight for him.

Gemma turned and followed Myrtle. "Troublesome witches. By the way, Aaron and I are taking you two out to dinner tonight."

Sonny looked up at him and batted his eyes. "Will you go to dinner with me and two annoying rabbits?"

He thought of the angry bunny on the trail the other night. "Can I eat them?"

"Wouldn't you rather have honey cakes?"

Leo's stomach growled again. "It's like you already know all my secrets. I'll do anything for honey cakes."

Sonny grinned and set his head on Leo's shoulder as they walked to the stairs. "It's kinda strange. I was so shy around you for months, but now, I feel like I've known you forever."

Mate, his bear grunted. Leo knew mates were a precious thing. His parents had told him their story over and over again. They had told all their kids about feeling like two halves finally becoming whole. He had thought it was mushy bullshit.

Now, though, he knew they hadn't been talking out their asses. In the shifter community, mated pairs moved fast, but witches were different. It took time for them to recognize their mates. Would Sonny want to mate with him? Leo's bear was positive he would, but Leo was a little more cautious.

I'll give it a few months, he decided. *That'll give Sonny time to settle into the idea.*

"Fair warning, I love cooking," Sonny said. "Baking is kinda my thing, but I make a great pot roast too. Do you have any allergies or dislike any foods?"

"Nope." Leo shook his head. "I don't have any allergies, and I like everything."

Sonny unlocked the door of his apartment and pulled Leo inside. "That makes things easier."

Leo sighed happily as he looked around Sonny's home. It was everything Leo's place wasn't. The layout was similar, with an open floor plan for the living room, dining room, and kitchen, but it was so warm and comfortable.

The hardwood floors were covered in thick, brightly colored rugs, and the walls were a deep plum. Sonny's furniture was big and overstuffed and looked like it would actually hold a man Leo's size.

Ferns and spirals of colorful glass hung from the ceiling in front of the windows, and a large plant rack with small pots of herbs sat in front of the largest living room window. Just like in Myrtle's home, herbs dried in the kitchen window and candles sat on every available surface.

Flufflepuff hopped off his shoulder and went to her cat condo in the corner of the living room.

Sonny bounced on his toes and watched Leo nervously. "Do you like it? I have three bedrooms, but one is my workroom. I know it's kind of messy, but I don't get a lot of visitors."

Leo cleared the lump from his throat. He didn't know what the hell was wrong with him. It was just Sonny's home. "I love it."

Sonny grinned. "Perfect. Have a seat, and I'll cook you breakfast."

Leo did as he was told and watched Sonny move around his kitchen. "Have you always liked cooking?"

"Yeah. My mom was a kitchen witch, and we knew early on that's where my affinity would go. She and I cooked together a lot."

Sonny sounded wistful, and Leo hurt for him. He

couldn't imagine not having his own mother, as annoying as she was.

"What about your dad?" Leo asked.

Sonny shrugged. "He's a hedge witch. Most of his time is spent with his scrying mirror and runes. He works with my mom on potions though. I learned a bit from him too." He gestured to a fragile, sea-green bowl sitting in the center of the coffee table. "I like using a scrying bowl, but I never got the hang of the runes."

Leo stroked a finger around the rim of the bowl. "My brother knows a hedge witch in law enforcement. He uses a pendulum in missing persons cases."

"Witches are a varied bunch." Sonny hummed as he mixed something in a large blue bowl. "Do you like working with your parents?"

Leo grinned as he leaned back in his chair. "Yeah. Dad loves the garage, and Mom and Coleen keep the auto shop running smooth. We all work there, but we have our preferences too. Niels likes working on motorcycles, Thorwald likes the luxury cars, and Rosemarie likes working on trucks."

"What about you?"

"I'm like Dad and my oldest brother, Burkhart. We like anything with a motor."

Sonny leaned over the bar separating the kitchen and living room and gave him a heated look. "I *really* like seeing you covered in grease."

Leo felt his face flush. Dillion had *not* liked the grease, but there was a world of difference between Sonny and Dillion.

Sonny tapped his chin and looked thoughtful for a

moment. "I think it's because I can tell you love your job, and I know you work hard at it." He shrugged. "Maybe I just have a mechanic fetish. Who knows?"

"I think I may have a kitchen witch fetish," Leo said, grinning.

~

A FEW HOURS LATER, SONNY TUCKED A BLANKET AROUND Leo. His bear was passed out on the couch, worn out from a restless night on a hard floor. Sonny's hand trembled as he smoothed his fingers over Leo's cheek.

Sonny kept his voice soft. "Flufflepuff, is this really happening? Is he really mine?"

"Meow." Flufflepuff hopped onto the couch and made her way to Leo's chest. She curled up in a ball and purred.

"You're right. He's right here in front of me." Sonny pressed his lips together to hold in a squeal. "I can't wait to learn everything about him, Flufflepuff. First, though, there's one very important question to ask."

Sonny gathered what he would need, then sat on the floor in front of his coffee table and poured water into his scrying bowl. Next, he put a small quartz crystal into the bowl and picked up his smudge stick. He had made one using lavender, heather, and meadowsweet specifically for this ritual.

He closed his eyes and focused his intention into the bundled herbs, then lit the end of the smudge stick. He waved it around his body, focusing on his head and his heart. Then he snuffed the flame out in a second, smaller bowl of sand.

Next, Sonny snapped his fingers and lit the two candles he had placed on either side of his scrying bowl. Then he closed his eyes again, falling into a meditative state that was as familiar and comfortable to him as sitting in his favorite chair.

He wasn't sure how much time had passed while his mind and heart cleared, but his soul knew when it was time. He opened his eyes and stared into the water of the scrying bowl. His sweet bear's face stared back at him from the water. *Mate!*

PART II
SUGAR COOKIES AND A WITCH'S LOVE

Holiday Omegas: Book Two

"If you two are mates, why hasn't he said anything?" Aaron asked. Sonny's best friend unloaded another bag of pillows and set them to the side.

Sonny unloaded his own bag and eyed the massive nest in the corner of Aaron's living room. Gemma, Aaron's mate, was expecting a kit and had ordered them to add to the nest while she was at work.

Flufflepuff, Sonny's familiar, sat on the back of the couch, white fluffy tail hanging down the cushion. The cat's green eyes blinked slowly, watching a bird through the window. Sonny took a cue from her and ignored Aaron.

He admired the new cuff bracelet his mate had given him last night. The silver cuff looked vintage and was shaped into intricate flowers with tiny ruby petals. *So pretty*. It went perfectly with his bright red sweater dress and thick grey leggings.

"Sonny," Aaron said, whacking him with a pillow. "If

you and Leo are mates, why hasn't he said anything? He should be acting overprotective and growly since you two haven't finished the claiming. Are you sure you're mates?"

Sonny scowled and retaliated, hitting Aaron with a pillow too. "Yes, I'm sure. Leo is really laid back and progressive. He probably understands that he doesn't have to be overprotective and growly."

Sonny and Leo had been dating for a month and a half now, ever since Halloween. They fit together like vanilla and sugar.

Aaron sucked his lip behind his big front teeth, eyes filling with worry. "Uh, that's not how shifters work, Sonny. Maybe—and please don't hate me for saying this—but maybe you two aren't mates. He's a bear shifter, and you're a witch. It's really unlikely."

Sonny narrowed his eyes and pummeled Aaron with the pillow until he fell to the floor. "Don't you say that! Leo is mine. I *know* he is."

The pillow split, and Aaron spat out feathers. "It's just that I've never heard of a bear mating a witch."

"It happens," Sonny said, studying his lovely bracelet again. "All species can mate; it's just not usual. Society doesn't like it, so families don't encourage it."

Aaron grabbed his leg, watching Sonny with big, sad eyes. "That's another thing. He hasn't told his family about you, Sonny. That's not normal. Mating is something to be celebrated. The day Gemma and I met, we knew we were mates. That next morning, I met her parents and she met mine. That's how shifters do things."

Sonny plopped onto the couch, shoulders slumping. "I don't know why he hasn't told them about me. Myrtle told me to be patient, but it *isn't* normal for a shifter. I know that."

Flufflepuff hopped from the back of the couch to his lap. Her paws kneaded the fabric of his sweater dress before she settled into a warm ball of floof.

Aaron grunted and crawled onto the couch from the floor. He wrapped an arm around Sonny's shoulders. "Maybe you should try scrying again?"

Sonny rolled his eyes. "It was as clear as day, Aaron. That's not going to change."

Aaron made a pained sound. "I hate even suggesting this, but do you think you ought to ask your father to scry and see if Leo really is your mate?"

Sonny made a face. "I will never be that desperate. You know how he is, Aaron."

Aaron winced. "Yeah. I do."

The apartment door opened, and Gemma walked in, eyes narrowing at the mess they had made. "What the hell?"

"Hey, baby," Aaron said, trying to look innocent. "We got those pillows you wanted."

Gemma growled. "Clean this mess up!"

Sonny stood, wobbling for a moment in his heeled boots. "Well, look at the time. I have to meet Miles. Sorry, Gem, but we got to train those baby witches up right."

He ran for the door. Gemma hissed at him as he ran past her. *Sounds more like a snake than a rabbit.*

He went to his apartment and found Miles waiting

in the living room. Sonny's apprentice had his books spread out on the floor in front of the balcony doors. His familiar, a puppy named Cookie, sprawled beside him, looking down at Miles's notebook.

A shot of warmth shot through Sonny. He remembered being in that exact position when he was an apprentice. Myrtle would make him a snack and talk to him about his day. *Damn, I love that woman.*

Miles looked up and grinned. "Hey, Sonny. Nice bracelet."

Sonny narrowed his eyes. "Hmm, you aren't *that* observant."

"Leo was worried about giving it to you," Miles said, sitting up and petting Flufflepuff when she crawled across his lap to get to Cookie. "He said it was his grandma's, and he really wanted you to like it."

Sonny cupped the bracelet. "He didn't tell me that." *There's a lot he doesn't tell me.*

Miles shrugged. "Don't look at me. What are we doing today?"

Sonny went to the kitchen and pointed at one of the seats at the bar. Miles hurried to sit down, eyes watching his every move.

Was I ever that eager? Sonny hid a smile and pulled his ingredients out of the cabinet. "Today we're going to talk about sugar."

Miles arched a brow. "Sugar? You use that a lot, and we're just now talking about it?"

Sonny gave him a look. "Don't get saucy with me. Sugar is one of the staples of many of my spells. Can you tell me why?"

Miles looked down at his training book and flipped through it a few times. "All I remember is the book said sugar was good at attracting stuff."

Sonny nodded. "That's why it's a good base. It attracts what you want it to. Now, plenty of witches use it to attract love or money, and that's okay. It's not a love potion, just a little push."

Miles side-eyed him. "I don't want anything to do with love potions."

Sonny snorted. "Good. Your cake pops did enough damage at Halloween." He shook his head. "What a lot of witches forget is that sugar attracts *whatever* you want. You could potentially want to attract a pack of wolves. I don't know."

Miles laughed. "That would be weird."

"Right?" Sonny smiled. "Now, the winter solstice is coming up, and I know we've talked about it before."

He waved his hand toward the living room. Holly and ivy plants were everywhere, and evergreen boughs and pinecones hung over the windows. Strings of lights were suspended from the ceiling, corner to corner, and candles covered every available surface. *Ritual, light, and rebirth.*

Finally, a sprig of mistletoe dangled over the door for luck, and a nice round wreath hung on the other side of the door, representing the continuity of life.

"Yeah, it's about celebrating light and quiet introspection, but also about home and family. It's not loud and boisterous like the spring solstice." Miles bit his lip. "A lot of non-witches celebrate it too and call it Christmas."

Sonny nodded. "Yes. That's mostly shifters and humans, but there's no harm in it." He waved at the Christmas tree in one of the corners of the living room. "Leo's family celebrates Christmas and most of the traditions fit right in with my own. You'll find many of the traditions and holidays different species celebrate overlap. We're all more alike than not."

Miles looked thoughtful for a minute, then nodded. "Okay. What's all this got to do with sugar?"

Sonny got a mixing bowl and set it in front of him. "We're going to make special winter solstice sugar cookies. Our purpose isn't to attract love or wealth, but to attract something far more important."

"What?" Miles leaned forward, eyes wide.

Sonny held up each ingredient. "Cloves for protection. A teensy, tiny bit of ginger for strength and new beginnings. A pinch of nutmeg for prosperity, and my favorite, vanilla, for happiness and self-love."

Miles nodded, face solemn. "And sugar, right?"

"Of course," Sonny said, grinning. "All of this is to attract something very important: good things for our family and home."

A FEW HOURS LATER, SONNY STIRRED THE SPAGHETTI sauce and breathed deeply, loving the scent of herbs and tomato. *Garlic for protection and health. Marjoram for courage. Oregano to strengthen bonds. Rosemary for love. Thyme for a little sexy magic, and parsley to enhance our naked fun time.*

He had just set the small kitchen table when Leo came in, using his own key to unlock the door. Sonny's bear was a big man with olive-colored skin and dark curly hair. His sweet smile made the whole damn room brighter.

Flufflepuff met Leo at the door and launched herself onto his shoulder. She curled into his neck and purred.

Leo patted her back and set his lunchbox on the counter. "That smells so good."

Sonny preened and practically danced in place. *My honey bear loves my cooking.* He knew he acted like an idiot around Leo, but there were only a handful of people in his life that had ever appreciated him. He couldn't help but get excited when his mate complimented him.

"Miles said he learned two spells tonight," Leo said and washed his hands in the kitchen sink. Sonny loved that Leo walked Miles home every day after their training. He had many a picture on his phone of his apprentice riding a huge brown bear with Cookie running around them.

"We had a lot to cover today," Sonny said and dipped under Leo's arm to hug him.

Leo instantly wrapped both arms around him and squeezed him tightly, lifting him from his feet. "You were supposed to relax on your day off."

Sonny battled Flufflepuff to bury his face against his mate's neck, enjoying Leo's scent mixed with smells from his family's auto shop. *Motor oil shouldn't smell so sexy.*

"Did you get any rest today?" Leo asked, spinning him around. "You work so hard, sunshine. You deserve time off."

Sonny smiled against Leo's neck. "I had some fun today. You ready for dinner?"

Leo's stomach growled. "That would be a yes."

They sat and filled their plates.

"How was the shop today?" Sonny asked, then took a bite.

Leo shrugged. "Like usual. Coleen brought in a new client. The guy collects motorcycles and needs some work done on a few of them. Niels thinks he's died and gone to heaven." He chewed happily for a moment before swallowing. "Can I take Flufflepuff with me to work tomorrow?"

Sonny almost choked on his bite of garlic bread. "You want to take my familiar with you to work?"

Leo flushed and looked at the table. "I don't have to. It was just an idea. I thought she might like hanging out in the front office."

Sonny glared at his cat, then forced himself to be an adult. "She can go. She'll probably have a lot of fun. I know she misses you during the day." *It doesn't matter that she gets to meet your family before I do. Really.*

Leo's face brightened again. "Thanks. I'll take good care of her. By the way, Gemma stopped me in the hall and told me you and Aaron got into a pillow fight today."

Sonny gave Leo his best innocent look and fluttered his eyes. "I told you I had some fun today."

Leo's laughter filled the room. "At least you didn't

turn his head into a pecan pie." His eyes heated. "Did you spell the spaghetti?"

Sonny wagged a finger at him. "You said I could spell dinner anytime. Reckless promise, wasn't it?"

Leo stood and set Flufflepuff on her cat stand before lifting Sonny from his chair and swinging him into his arms. He headed for the bedroom. "Dinner will be here when we get back, sunshine."

Moments later, Sonny braced himself on the bed as Leo pounded into him from behind. The feel of his mate filling him to the brink of pain always broke him into a thousand pieces. When Leo kissed the back of his neck and mumbled sweet nonsense words, the pieces reformed, stronger than ever.

THE NEXT MORNING, SONNY SETTLED HIS HEAD ON HIS fist and watched the man stretched out beside him sleep. His mate was a sexy fucker, even if he stole most of the covers.

Leo's chest rose and lowered as he breathed, and Sonny couldn't resist threading his fingers through the bear shifter's thick chest hair. His bear was a bear in more than one way.

Sonny snickered at his pun. *I'm so punny.*

Leo snuffled in his sleep, and Sonny felt a burst of happiness shoot through him. This was his mate—the one man that was his perfect soulmate. *Fuck Aaron. I know Leo's my mate.*

He leaned over and buried his face against Leo's

neck, moving his naked body closer to the warmth of the big alpha. His ass was still a bit tender from the night before, but there were other ways to satisfy his hunger. *If I can get my honey bear to wake up.*

Sonny licked and nipped Leo's neck while one hand strolled south to stroke Leo's long, thick dick to life.

Leo moaned and his sleepy brown eyes opened. "Sonny?"

Sonny kissed him softly, then pushed the covers back. "Can I?"

Leo chuckled and raised his hands over his head. "Anytime, sunshine."

Sonny trailed his lips down Leo's furry chest, one hand kneading the muscles under the hair. He bit a nipple, then licked it before doing the same to the other one. He took his time pressing kisses to Leo's soft stomach. His bear was a little self-conscious, but damn, did his belly look good on him.

When his mouth reached Leo's dick, Sonny hummed in pleasure. His mate had enough girth that Sonny needed both hands to fully hold him. He sat up and started working his mate's dick, licking his lips when he saw precum drip from the tip.

Sonny leaned down and swallowed the head, sucking gently, while he stroked the rest of Leo's hard length. Steadily, he took more and more of Leo's dick in his mouth, sucking hard as he went.

Leo's big hands gently cupped Sonny's head. He looked up, enjoying the sight of his alpha's face flushed with arousal.

Sonny pressed his own dick against the bed, hips

moving in rhythm with his strokes. *Damn, my honey bear tastes so good.* He worked Leo's dick for a while, then moved onto his balls, sucking first one, then the other into his mouth.

"Fuck, Sonny!" Leo's grip on his head tightened, then he was spurting between them. Sonny barely closed his eyes in time.

Leo panted as he grabbed the sheet, wiping at Sonny's face. "I'm so sorry."

Sonny stifled a giggle and rolled over. "Finish me?"

Leo's eyes grew heavy, and he looked so pleased at the sight of Sonny's hard dick. "With pleasure."

It didn't take long for Sonny to come, and Leo swallowed it all. Sonny patted his mate's head. "Thank you, honey bear."

CHAPTER 8

*L*eo kissed Sonny goodbye and tried not to smile when his witch glared at Flufflepuff. Leo knew Sonny was ready to take the next step in their relationship, but he was nervous his family would ruin the warm happiness Leo had found. Flufflepuff was a test.

He picked up his lunch and Flufflepuff's carrier and leash. It had snowed each night for a week now, so it was too cold to walk Sonny's familiar to the auto shop. He put her into her carrier and strapped her into the seat of his truck.

Rocchi's Garage was a short distance away. He saw his parents' car parked next to his sister Coleen's. Those three were always the first to arrive. Then came Leo, Burkhart, Rosemarie, Thorwald, and finally, Niels.

Leo breathed deeply, then let it out in a rush. "Okay, Flufflepuff. This is the first test. I'm sorry I'm using you, but I need to make sure they're ready for Sonny.

They tease constantly, and I don't want to upset my sunshine."

Flufflepuff meowed pitifully from her carrier.

"Oh, I'll let you out. Sorry, Fluff." Leo opened the carrier and snuggled with the cat for a minute. Sonny might be jealous of his familiar, but he had made sure she was dressed nicely in her Hufflepuff cat sweater.

He grabbed the lunch Sonny had packed him and left his truck.

Coleen was already straightening up the waiting room and wiping down the front desk. She looked up when he came in. "Why do you have a cat with you?"

"This is Flufflepuff, and she's going to be visiting us today," Leo said, voice formal.

Coleen tucked a strand of black hair behind her ear and narrowed her eyes on him. His sisters were beautiful women with olive skin, black hair, and full figures. They were also as different as night and day. Coleen was a bit prissy and definitely a diva.

"What's going on?" she asked.

Leo shrugged. "Flufflepuff is a good friend, and I want her to see where I work."

"Okay," Coleen said, drawing the word out. She looked over her shoulder and shouted. "Mom, Leo's being weird."

"Just ignore him, Coleen," Leo's mother, Katrin, yelled back. "I'm working on the books and don't have time for your shit."

Coleen grumbled but looked back at Leo. "Fine. The cat can stay up here with me, but if it gets annoying, I'm bringing it to the garage."

Leo sniffed and hugged Flufflepuff. "You fail, Coleen. Flufflepuff is my friend and you've insulted her."

Coleen rubbed her face. "And they call me the drama queen."

"She'll stay in the garage with me." Leo turned on his heel and marched to the breakroom. He set Flufflepuff down and put his lunch in the fridge. He loved that damn spaghetti and hoped his siblings didn't steal it. Italian food was a favorite in the Rocchi household. His dad's grandparents were Italian and had passed down their love of food to each family member along with the Rocchi name.

"What do you have there?" Leo's dad, Jesse, asked over his shoulder.

Leo jumped, then spun around. "Leave my lunch alone."

"You've been bringing in quality food for a while now," Jesse said, eying him suspiciously. "Where are you getting it from?"

Leo cleared his throat. "I'd like you to meet Flufflepuff. She's a friend of mine and will be visiting today."

Flufflepuff tilted her head and watched Jesse. "Meow."

Jesse made a face. "Does it have fleas? I don't want fleas in the garage, Leo. Do you think we'd attract the fleas when we're shifted?"

Flufflepuff's green eyes narrowed.

Leo picked her up and stroked her head. "You've

failed, Father. Flufflepuff is my friend and you've been very rude. Does she look like she has fleas?"

"*Father*? Since when do you call me *Father*?" Jesse rolled his eyes and shouted over his shoulder. "Katrin, your son is being weird!"

"Damn it, I can't help that Leo is weird. He's family, so deal with it," Katrin yelled back. "I'm working on the books. Leave me alone."

Leo shook his head, giving his dad a disappointed look. "I expected better from you." He left the breakroom and went to his station. It was the farthest from the office. "I'm sorry, Fluff. I knew Coleen and Mom might be difficult, but I really thought Dad would at least say hi to you."

He set the cat on top of one of his work tables, and Flufflepuff yawned and settled down for a nap.

Burkhart came in shortly after.

"Burk, this is Flufflepuff. She's my friend and visiting for the day." Leo waved to Flufflepuff.

Burkhart blinked at the sleeping cat. "Uh, hi?"

Leo smiled wide. "You pass, Burk. I always knew you were my favorite sibling."

Thorwald yawned as he walked past. "Who's the cat?"

"Flufflepuff," Leo said, scratching her head. "She's my friend."

"Whatever." Thorwald shrugged and went to his station.

"You fail, Thor," Leo said, curling his lip. "You're dead to me."

Rosemarie stopped at his station. "Wow. That's harsh."

"Rosemarie." Leo nodded at his sister. "This is Flufflepuff, a dear friend of mine."

She reached out and let Fluff sniff her fingers before petting Sonny's familiar. "Sweet cat. Does your apartment building let you have pets?"

Leo leaned over and kissed her forehead. "You pass, Rose. You're my favorite sibling."

"Hey," Burkhart said, looking up from arranging his tools. "I thought I was."

Leo opened his garage door and the first car pulled in for an oil change. "You both are. I can have two favorites."

Rosemarie laughed and went to her station.

Leo was halfway through the first job when Niels ran in, tugging on his coveralls. "Neils! This is my friend, Flufflepuff."

Niels gave him a bewildered look. "What? Are you high?" He looked at Flufflepuff. "Wait, is that cat wearing a sweater? Am I high?"

"You failed." Leo shook his head sadly. "You're dead to me. Go away."

Niels shrugged and ran to his station. "You're so weird."

Leo finished the oil change, then took a second to pet Flufflepuff. "I'm sorry my family has treated you so poorly. You're a good cat and a good familiar. You deserve better."

"She's a familiar?" Burkhart asked behind him. "Who's her witch?"

Leo jumped, startled. "What are you talking about? There's a customer waiting on you, Burk. We don't have time for this."

Burkhart eyed him suspiciously. "You *are* acting weird."

Thorwald walked by singing a Bette Midler song at the top of his lungs, earbuds in. Leo gave Burkhart a flat look. "*I'm* the weird one?"

Several oil changes and three tire rotations later, Leo wiped his hands on a rag and picked up Flufflepuff. "Lunch time, Fluff. I packed some treats so you won't feel out of place."

Rocchi's Garage always closed from one to two so that everyone could eat lunch together. *Time for test number two.*

He walked into the breakroom and froze when all of his siblings turned to glare at him. "What?"

"What the hell was in that spaghetti, Leo?" Coleen asked, hands propped on her ample hips.

Leo shrugged. "Stuff that goes in spaghetti."

"Dad ate it, then started kissing Mom," Niels said, slightly green. "I mean like *real* deep kisses. I heard things and now I'm traumatized."

"Dad ate my spaghetti?" Leo frowned, shoulders slumping. He'd been looking forward to his lunch.

"They're having sex in the office," Thorwald said, appalled. "We all know it. They know that we know, but they don't care. What the fuck was in that spaghetti?"

"What makes you think it had to be the spaghetti?"

Leo said, texting an order to the pizza place around the corner. He was hungry, damn it.

"He ate your lunch, then a second later we could practically see the hearts in his eyes. He went right for Mom," Rosemarie said, shuddering. "She giggled, Leo. Giggled."

"It's nothing to worry about," Leo said, face flushing. "Just a little spell to set the mood."

Burkhart watched Flufflepuff in consideration. "Hmm, so you bring a spelled lunch to work along with a witch's familiar, who also happens to be your friend."

Thorwald leaned forward, arms folded on the table. "We've scented the new man on you, Leo. We've just tried to be polite and not bug you about it. Are you dating a witch?"

Coleen's eyes widened. "That's it, isn't it? You're dating a witch. That's wicked cool, bro."

"I thought you wanted to settle down," Niels said, looking confused. "Dillion was a douchebag, but you'll find a nice omega bear one day."

Leo almost bit his tongue off, but he managed not to strangle Niels. *I've already found my nice omega mate. I don't need a bear. I have my witch.*

"Hey, there's no harm in having a little fun before you settle down," Thorwald said, laughing. "I've always wanted to date a vampire. I hear that when they drink from you during sex—"

Rosemarie covered his mouth. "No sex talk from you."

Niels bit his lip. "It just seems like Leo really wants the whole settling down thing, so it's not smart to date a witch while you wait for your fated mate to come along."

Coleen looked thoughtful. "You have a point. Leo, you shouldn't be playing the field. You're not a manwhore like Thor. You're sensitive and caring. Look, I know a couple of omegas that I think you'd like. I've been holding off on matchmaking because I thought you were still recovering from Dillion, but clearly you're ready to get back out there."

Leo settled Flufflepuff on his shoulder and grabbed her treats from his open lunch box. "You all fail, big time. I'm eating lunch with Flufflepuff in my truck."

A few minutes later, his pizza was delivered and he had the truck nice and warm. He gave Flufflepuff some treats and took a bite of his first slice before he dialed a number on his phone.

"Hey, baby boy. How's it going?" His grandma's voice was a soothing balm on the nerves his siblings had irritated.

"Hey, Grandma." Leo took another bite and swallowed. "I don't think the family is ready to hear about Sonny. They can't even consider that my mate could be a witch."

"They're a pack of knuckleheads, that's for sure," Janine said. "I love each and every one of you, but y'all can be dense. Now, did you actually tell them Sonny is your mate?"

Leo shared a look with Flufflepuff. "Uh, no. You know how they are. They'll get all rowdy and opinionated. I don't want him running away."

"I can't wait to meet this witch that has you all

aflutter." He could hear the smile in her voice. "You've invited him to come to the farm, right?"

"Not yet." Leo sighed. "I wanted to see how things went today before I did it. Do you think everyone will behave?"

"If they don't, I'll roast them in the oven for dinner," she said. Leo was a little worried she meant that. "Are you sure the best way to introduce him to your parents is at Christmas? You know your aunt, uncles, and cousins will be here too."

"That's why I think it will be best," Leo said. "This way, Mom will be distracted with Aunt Tula and Dad will be going bear outside with the uncles."

"Hmm, I'm not convinced, but I'm too excited to meet him to bother trying to talk you out of it." Janine was quiet for a moment. "His family really won't mind?"

"Nope," Leo said. "I told you about his parents and grandparents. Normally, he'd go to the coast and spend winter solstice with Myrtle and her sister Hester."

"What about that rabbit of his?" Janine asked.

Leo smiled. "Aaron and Gemma split the holidays between their parents' homes."

"Okay. I just don't want nobody spending Christmas alone."

"I love you, Grandma."

"Love you too, sweetie. Eat your lunch and go give your family hell. Tell my son he better get in shape before I see him. I'm not afraid to whomp him."

"Yes, ma'am." He hung up and smiled at Flufflepuff. "Grandma and Grandpa are on our side, Fluff. If I can just ease everyone together without Sonny thinking we're a bunch of maniacs, I'll be good."

~

LEO WATCHED SONNY CLOSELY. HIS WITCH SAT ON HIS lap on the couch, bundled in a cozy blanket and Leo's favorite hoodie. "So, what do you say?"

Sonny's eyes were wide with hope. "You want me to go with you to your grandparents for the winter solstice?"

"Yeah. We do Christmas, but Grandma knows there's a few things you'll want to add to it. She's looking forward to getting to know you." Leo could have kicked himself when Sonny's eyes watered.

"She really wants to meet me?"

"She sure does." Leo cupped Sonny's face and kissed him. "That's her bracelet I gave you, you know. She sent it to me to give to you when I told her about you."

Sonny squealed and bounced in Leo's lap. "Miles told me it was hers. I'm glad she wants to meet me."

Leo grunted. "Watch the goods, sunshine."

"Sorry." Sonny squeezed his cheeks and kissed him. "You know I like your goods."

"That you do."

Sonny bit his lip. "I can tone it down while we're there and just wear my guy stuff. I've been digging my jeans and your hoodies lately anyway."

"No." Leo shook his head, brow furrowing. "You dress however you want to dress. Grandma and Grandpa asked me all kinds of questions because they

73

don't know anyone that's genderfluid, but they want you to be comfortable. To be honest, Grandma has a few more pieces of jewelry for you. She's been hoarding all kinds of things for years and loves passing it on to family."

Sonny gave him a serious look. "Am I family?"

Leo kissed him slowly, savoring the warm taste of Sonny's lips. "You're my family, Sonny."

CHAPTER 9

Sonny waved goodbye to Miles and his parents after dropping off presents at their house. One thing Christmas and winter solstice had in common was giving gifts. It was a nice way to show your loved ones that you cared.

Miles would appreciate Sonny's old grimoire. A witch needed to explore their personal magic and creating grimoires was part of that. Miles would like the spells Sonny had created when he was his age.

He had already given gifts to Aaron and Gemma, but he still needed to say goodbye to Myrtle. It was strange not spending the holiday with his friend and mentor, but finally meeting Leo's family was too good to pass up.

He knocked on her door. "Open up, woman! It's Santa Sonny."

Myrtle opened the door and glared at him. She was still dressed in her nightgown and robe. "It's too early for this shit, Sonny."

"I'm leaving in fifteen minutes," he said, pouting. "Don't you want to say goodbye?"

"You're going away for a week, not a year." Myrtle huffed and pulled him into a hug. "I'll miss you, boy-o, but I'm glad you're moving forward with your cat-bear. I expected the two of you to be married with ten kids by now."

"It's been a month and a half, Myrtle," Sonny said dryly. "Plus, I'm not having ten fucking kids, woman. Don't put that out into the universe."

Myrtle cackled. "Well, when you eventually move in together in ten years, I suggest you combine your apartments. His is right below yours. We could add a stairway and do a little remodeling."

Sonny hugged her again and kissed the side of her head. "You're the best mother, you know that, right?"

Her thin arms tightened around him. "You're a good son." She pushed him back. "Now get out of here. Toddlebug and I have to pack for the beach. Hester says it's cold, but it ain't snowing there so she don't know shit."

Sonny rolled his eyes. Myrtle and her sister were too much alike and were constantly competing with one another.

"I love you. Take your present." He shoved a wrapped box at her. "Goodbye."

"Hold it, I got yours around here somewhere." She turned and set the box on a side table.

Sonny shook his head as he looked around her cluttered apartment. "Do we need to have an intervention, Myrtle? Your clutter multiples every five seconds."

"Don't you get uppity, witch." Myrtle shot him a hard look. "Half this shit is stuff for the store. We need to expand." She held up a small bag. "This is your Christmas gift. It's a potion of my own making. It's a calming potion. You can bake it into anything you want."

Sonny blinked. "Seriously? I thought you said those were too expensive to make and pot does the same thing."

"That's why it's a gift, goober." She shook the bag. "Now take it and get moving. It's been more than fifteen minutes."

"Shit." Sonny grabbed the bag and hugged Myrtle one more time. "Tell Hester I said hi." He ran up the stairs and hurried into his apartment.

Leo sat on the couch, Flufflepuff in his lap.

"I'm sorry. My bags are ready. I was just saying goodbye to everyone, and then Aaron wanted me to try this new videogame. I lost track of time."

Leo smiled. "It's no big deal. I already loaded your bags. You know it's just for the week, right? That's six nights and seven days."

"Yes, but you said to wear whatever I want and sometimes I want to wear a skirt or leggings, sometimes I want my jeans and hoodie, and sometimes I want to mix the two." He waved his hands around his head. "Welcome to genderfluidity."

Leo laughed. "Okay. Luckily, I pack light, so we balance out. I packed Flufflepuff's bag too."

Sonny looked around the kitchen, then gave Leo a look. "Did you get my insulated bag?"

Leo blinked, eyes widening in innocence. "What insulated bag?"

Sonny put his hands on his hips and stared down his nose. "The one full of honey cakes."

Leo shrugged. "I may have seen it, and I may have eaten all of the honey cakes. Maybe."

"All of them?" Sonny snorted and quickly packed some ingredients. "I'll have to make a fresh batch when we get there."

"Was that supposed to be enough for everyone?" Leo looked doubtful. "We may need to stop at the store for more stuff. There's a lot of us, sunshine."

An hour later, they were on the road in Leo's truck. Their bags were in the back with a cover over the bed since it was snowing again.

Sonny watched the city slip by as they entered the suburbs. "Sometimes I wish I had a house so I could have a garden in the yard."

"Is that something you want one day?" Leo asked, glancing at him before his eyes went back to the road.

"I don't know. I'm no garden witch," Sonny said. "That apartment is my home, and I love everything about it. It's *my* space. A place where I'm safe and can just be myself with no one judging me."

Leo reached over Flufflepuff's carrier and took his hand. "I know how you feel. Your apartment is my safe place too. I'm learning how to be comfortable with myself."

Oh, honey bear, let me be your mate. Sonny somehow

kept the words in and reminded himself to keep it simple. He didn't want to scare Leo away with his desperation. "It's not my apartment anymore, is it? It's become *our* home." *Way to keep it simple, Sonny.*

Leo grinned. "Yeah. It is. Does this mean I can move in?"

Sonny told his heart to stop beating so fast. He didn't want to have a heart attack. "Yes. We'll move everything as soon as we get back home."

"Myrtle won't like having to find another tenant." Leo didn't sound all that concerned. The bear almost seemed smug.

Sonny thought about her suggestion. "She might like us to renovate a little and join our apartments."

Leo looked shocked. "Seriously?"

"Well, yeah. We could redo some space and have more room and a larger kitchen." Sonny liked the thought of that. He liked the thought of Leo sharing his home. "I would tie you to a chair and make you stay with me forever if it wasn't illegal." *Shit, did I say that aloud?*

Leo snorted, then started laughing. "Bondage fantasies? I'll try it with you, sunshine."

Sonny flushed and buried his nose in the bright red scarf wrapped loosely around his neck. Today he was feeling a bit more androgynous than usual, so he wore fashionably torn jeans, low-heeled boots, and a cream-colored sweater. His cuff bracelet caught the light and he admired it again. Leo's grandma had good taste.

"Tell me more about your family," Sonny said,

wishing he had put Flufflepuff next to the door so he could sit beside Leo.

"My parents are Katrin and Jesse. They met when my mom was in school. My dad lived on his parents' farm and worked in a small auto shop in the closest town. Mom was on a road trip with her friends when their car broke down."

"Aww." Sonny's bottom lip popped out and his eyes widened. "That sounds like a romance movie."

Leo chuckled. "They met and knew they were mates right away. Mom's parents weren't thrilled. They're from Germany and had wanted her to marry a bear from their homeland. They weren't too keen on an American."

"That didn't stop her," Sonny said and stuck his fingers in Flufflepuff's carrier to pet her side.

"Nope. They mated the next day and it was done."

"Aaron says shifters don't do weddings," Sonny said. He heard the sadness in his own voice but couldn't help it. Handfasting was an important tradition for witches.

"No, we normally just mate." Leo looked completely unconcerned while Sonny was quietly dying inside. He had designed a handfasting dress when he was twelve, and Aaron had promised to dance the bunny boogie at his wedding. "Mom's parents moved back to Germany when I was six. They're nice and all, but we aren't close. Dad's parents, on the other hand, would keep us in their pockets if they could."

Sonny forced his attention away from his dashed dreams. "You said they weren't happy when your parents moved to the city."

"Nope, but they accepted it." Leo shrugged. "That's what parents do, right? They let Dad and Mom start their own dream. Grandpa and Grandma were raised in the country and always planned on farming. That was their dream."

"What's your dream?" Sonny leaned over Fluff's carrier and watched his mate carefully.

Leo eyed him in amusement. "I'm simple enough. I want to work at the garage and have a family of my own. What about you? You love Myrtle's shop, don't you?"

Sonny nodded. "I guess I'm also simple. I want to run the shop and help people. I want my own family too." *We fit perfectly, honey bear. Be my mate.* "What about your brothers and sisters?"

"Coleen is great with the customers. She's a beta and loves socializing of all kinds. She has a good head for marketing too. Rosemarie is her twin and an alpha. She's the exact opposite in personality. She likes nothing better than being alone with her head in the engine of a truck. Then there's Thorwald. He's older than me, but younger than the twins. He's an alpha and loves the omegas. Mom and Dad worry that he'll never want to settle down. Then there's Niels. He's the youngest and the only omega. He loves working at the shop, but he writes too. One day, he'll be famous."

Sonny counted in his head. "There's one more, right?"

"Burkhart," Leo said. "He's the eldest and an alpha."

"What's he like?" Sonny watched his mate, puzzled. Leo had been open about the others.

Leo was quiet for a moment. "You have to promise not to fall in love with him."

Sonny covered his mouth to hide his laughter, but it spilled over anyway.

"You laugh, but it happens all the time," Leo said, making an annoyed sound. "He's a lot like me in that he's laid back, but he has fucking abs of steel."

Sonny leaned back in his seat and cackled like the witch he was. *I need to stop spending so much time with Myrtle.*

"I'm serious," Leo said, shaking his head. "He's all quiet and brooding too. Omegas go crazy for him."

Sonny wheezed for a moment, then caught his breath. "I promise I won't fall in love with your brother."

"Thorwald too. He's good-looking and takes after Mom's side of the family, so he's blond and buff."

Sonny snickered. "Blond and buff."

"Do you know how many boyfriends I've lost to them?"

Sonny sobered, frowning. "They took your boyfriends?"

"Well, they didn't really take them," Leo said slowly. "They never dated them, but four of my past boyfriends broke up with me in the hopes of hooking either Burk or Thor."

"Oh," Sonny said. "As long as they aren't being cruel. I'd have had to try out Myrtle's favorite curse on them."

"Turning their dicks into snakes?" Leo shuddered. "I love her, but Myrtle scares me sometimes."

"I promise I won't fall in love with your brothers,"

Sonny said. "I make no promises about falling in love with your Grandma. If she gives me pretty, shiny things, I'm hers."

Leo smiled fondly. "I'll share you with her."

Sonny bit his lip. "How do your parents and siblings feel about me?"

Leo watched the road in silence, eyes wide.

"Leo?" Sonny narrowed his eyes. "How do they feel about me?"

"Uh, well… The thing is…" Leo trailed off.

"Leo!"

"They don't know," Leo said, squeezing the steering wheel. "I haven't told them about you."

Sonny felt tears fill his eyes. He sank into the seat. "Are you ashamed of me?"

"What?" Leo cursed and started weaving through traffic. "No, I'm not ashamed of you, sunshine." He pulled to the side of the road and put the truck in park before turning to Sonny. "I've been worried my family will scare you off. Dillion never took their teasing well, and he thought they were too lowbrow or something like that."

Sonny sniffled and punched Leo's arm. "I'm not Dillion. He's an idiot, but I'm not."

Leo reached over the carrier and cupped his face. "Swear you won't run once you meet my family. Please?"

"I swear I won't run," Sonny said. "If they're truly terrible, I'll turn them into pecan pies, but I won't leave you."

Leo's smile was shaky, but he pulled back into

traffic. "I'll do my best to make sure you don't regret it, sunshine."

By the time they got to the farm, Sonny was tired of looking at the snow-covered trees. There were too many of them. "I hate trees."

Leo chuckled. "How can you say that? You're a witch and love all that nature stuff."

"Trees ate my mother." Sonny yawned. "Plus, they're boring."

"Wow. Here I thought your mother lived a few blocks away," Leo said dryly. "I never knew of this tragedy you speak of."

"Seriously though," Sonny said, glaring at the woods around them. "Gnomes live in forests and they kinda hate witches. At least that's what Myrtle told me."

Leo turned onto a long, rough driveway. "Be honest with me. Besides your trips to Myrtle's sister, have you ever left the city?"

"Once." Sonny bounced in his seat as the truck hit a particularly deep hole. "My parents made me go to a summer solstice camp for kids. It sucked big time. I found all the poison ivy patches and a racoon tried to eat Flufflepuff."

Leo pulled the truck to a stop outside of a large farmhouse decorated in lights. "How old *is* Fluff?"

"I got her when I was nine," Sonny said. "Familiars live longer than regular pets."

"Oh," Leo said, then frowned. "Shit, here they come."

In seconds, the truck was surrounded by big, dark-haired bears. *Oh, there's a blond. Must be Thorwald.* "There's more than five of them."

"My cousins are in there too, along with my aunts and uncles."

"Leo," Sonny said, growling. "I haven't even met your parents yet. Won't they be mad at you for springing this on them at the last minute?"

"They'll be fine, sunshine," Leo said, giving him a nervous smile. He glared and beat on the windshield when one of the smaller ones slid onto the hood of the truck. "Go away!"

"Hi." A woman appeared at Sonny's door and opened it. She unbuckled his seatbelt and picked him up out of the car, carrying him in her arms. "I like your boots. Are you Leo's witch? You made our parents traumatize us."

"Damn, Leo," Thorwald said, opening Leo's door and punching his shoulder. "Your witch is hot. Nice job."

The largest of the bears raised his hands in the air. "I'm the witch's secret Santa! I have the perfect gift for him."

"That's not fair, Burk," an older woman said. She stood on the porch and watched them all in amusement. "You were already given a secret Santa, and I just happen to have a gift for Sonny."

"You know him?" a tall blonde woman asked. She was one of only two blondes. *Leo's mom. Katrin.*

"Yes, I do." The older woman smiled at him. "I'm Janine, sweetheart. Leo's grandma. That's Rosemarie who's carrying you. Bring him into the house, Rose. It's cold out here."

"I have his cat," Burkhart said, holding up Flufflepuff's carrier. "It's cool. We met a few days ago."

The man beside Janine smiled at Sonny. "I'm Ronald, Leo's grandpa. Welcome to our home, Sonny."

CHAPTER 10

*L*eo watched the door while Sonny unpacked. He didn't trust that his family wouldn't chase them into the bedroom and ask more questions or say rude things.

"I can't believe your sister carried me into the house." Sonny snickered and hung a dress in the closet. "What do you think Burkhart is going to give me for Christmas? How can he possibly have a gift for me without knowing I was coming?"

Leo ran his tongue over his teeth and narrowed his eyes. Did the doorknob just twitch?

"It's just noon. What do you think we'll do today? Christmas is a few days away, but the winter solstice is tomorrow. I didn't see a tree downstairs. I thought your family always did a tree. Oh, do you think they'll mind if I do a few blessings and hang some mistletoe?"

Leo smiled as Sonny rambled. He'd noticed his mate's nerves, but Sonny was handling it well. Dillion would have already run for the hills or would have been complaining non-stop. *My sunshine isn't Dillion.*

"I really like Janine and Ronald." Sonny slipped under his arm and hugged him. "I wish my grandparents were as accepting as yours."

Leo closed his eyes and snuggled his witch. "They're not so bad." The door flew open and Rosemarie and Niels came in. "These two, on the other hand…"

"Can you make a potion to turn someone green?" Niels asked, sitting on the bed. "I'm asking for a friend."

"Forget him," Rosemarie said, shoving Niels to the side to steal his spot. "He's just mad at Thor. I have a more important question. There's this omega named Kate that just started working at the coffee shop down the street. She's a black bear shifter. Can you do a spell to see if she likes me? I think she may be my mate."

Leo's mouth dropped open. "Rosemarie, that's big. Do you really think she's your mate?"

His sister flushed, then shrugged. "Maybe. I haven't spent a lot of time with her, and you know my nose is a bit funny."

"What do mean?" Sonny asked, frowning.

"Had a birth defect," Rosemarie said gruffly. "My nose is about as good as yours. Shifters sense their mates through scent."

Sonny moved to the bed and set Flufflepuff in Rosemarie's lap. "When we're back in town, I'll do a scrying for you. I'll need something that belongs to her. A hair would be best."

"Thanks, Sonny." Rosemarie stroked Flufflepuff's

back. "Leo, Dad wanted me to tell you we're hunting the tree in about thirty minutes."

Sonny looked delighted. "We're actually going to hunt a Christmas trees in the woods?"

Niels snorted. "No. They all get drunk and go to the Christmas tree farm down the road to get a tree. Rosemarie gets to be one of the three designated drivers this year."

Sonny looked a little nervous. "Is there a gnome village nearby? Will the Christmas tree farm be safe?"

Rosemarie turned her laugh into a cough. "There is a small gnome village north of here. Please tell me you aren't afraid of gnomes. They're sweet and adorable."

Sonny shuddered and Leo hugged him again, doing his best to hide his laughter.

Niels grinned. "You should stay with me and make Christmas cookies. No gnomes here."

Sonny smiled shyly. "Okay."

"Now, about turning people green?"

"What exactly did Thorwald do to you?" Sonny asked, raising a brow. "There are a lot of things we can do that may be better revenge than just turning him green."

Rosemarie grinned. "On that note, Leo and I are going to start preparing for the hunt."

"By that, she means start in on Grandma's eggnog." Leo kissed Sonny's cheek. "You sure you're okay staying behind?"

"Of course." Sonny looked down his nose. "I'm an adult and perfectly capable of making some cookies with your brother."

Leo followed Rosemarie out the door. "Niels will watch out for him, right?"

Rosemarie blew her bangs out of her eyes. "You worry too much. He's really nice, Leo. You shouldn't be jerking him around. What are you going to do when you meet that perfect omega bear and mate? Sonny has the feels for ya. I can tell."

Leo frowned. He needed to tell them that Sonny was his mate, but he hadn't even talked about it with Sonny. It didn't seem right.

"That's my worry too." Katrin waited for them at the bottom of the stairs, arms crossed. "You haven't told us anything about this person, Leo."

"Bah, you worry too much Katrin." Ronald waved her away and handed Leo a large glass of eggnog. "We need to go get the tree. Your grandma is itching to decorate it tonight."

A few eggnogs later and Leo wasn't worrying too much. Several Rocchi family members wandered the Christmas tree farm, looking for the perfect one. Loud laughter and mock fights drew the glares of the owners, but Grandpa smoothed things over as usual.

"Bro, your witch is so hot," Thorwald said, swaying slightly. "Damn, those legs of his go on for miles. He's short, but still manages to have long legs. How is that possible?"

Leo gritted his teeth and forced back his growl. He propped himself up against one of the trees, dizzy for a moment.

Burkhart hugged one of the other trees. "This tree is too skinny. I like some padding on my trees."

Thorwald hugged the tree next. "Yeah, way too skinny." He looked at Leo. "Your witch has some nice, lean muscles on him too, but that ass? Damn, that ass is perfectly plump."

Burkhart shoved Thorwald out of the way and hugged the next tree. "This is it. This is our tree!"

Thorwald hugged the tree too. "Oh yeah. These are some nice branches."

"Dad," Burkhart yelled. "We found our tree."

Jesse, Ronald, and a few of Leo's uncles came through the trees. "What are you boys doing?" Jesse asked, shaking his head.

"This is our tree, Dad." Burkhart hugged it again. "I can feel it."

A bear walked past them, grumbling softly. Another one, smaller than the first, pranced past, shaking his head.

"Damn it, Ronald. There are six bears wandering around." The owner shook his fist at them. "I told you before. If any of you break one of the trees rubbing your back on it, you have to buy it. I wish y'all hibernated in the winter."

Rosemarie jogged over. "We may have already broken three."

"We'll round everyone up," Ronald said, slapping his friend on the back. "We'll take this tree that my grandsons are hugging and the three we ruined."

The owner shook his head. "You are annoying as hell, but you do make me money. Move your drunk asses to the empty plot next door while I ring you up."

"Snowball fight," Burkhart yelled and started

91

stumbling toward the field. "Grandpa, I'm kicking your ass."

"I'd love to see you try, boy," Ronald said and ran after Burkhart.

"I'd love to see Sonny naked," Thorwald said, stumbling into Leo. "You're a lucky bear, bro."

Leo pushed him away, frowning.

Jesse wrapped his arm around Leo's shoulders and steered him toward the field. "I've been meaning to ask. That man you brought, he dresses a little strange, doesn't he? I know you boys are gay, but that doesn't mean you gotta wear girly clothes and jewelry."

Leo's face went hot, and he shoved his dad away. A cold snowball hit Jesse in the face, startling both of them.

"That's just stupid talk, Jesse," Ronald said. "Sonny's genderfluid and wears whatever he feels like wearing. Nothing wrong with that."

"Huh." Jesse wiped snow from his face. "I've heard of that. Does that mean I shouldn't call him *him*? Damn it, I already messed it up."

"Janine says he uses male pronouns," Ronald said, then looked at Leo. "That's right, isn't it?" He stumbled into his son and stuffed a handful of snow down the back of his coat.

Jesse yelped and danced around.

Leo smothered his laughter. "Yeah, Grandpa. He says male pronouns are usually easier for people to remember so he goes by them."

Ronald frowned. "But is that what *he* wants?" He rubbed his eyes. "I think I drank too much."

"I'll remember, son," Jesse said, shaking the snow out of his coat. "I'll ogle it."

Rosemarie pushed their cousins toward the field. "You mean google it, Dad."

"I'm gonna ogle Sonny when we get home," Thorwald said, smirking.

Burkhart tackled him, and the two rolled around in the snow.

Rosemarie gave Leo a wide-eyed look. "You okay there, Leo? I've never heard you growl like that before. You're the most laid back of us."

"I'm fine," he said through gritted teeth. "When are we going home?"

"Looks like the trees have been loaded," Ronald said. "Let's get you back to your witch."

CHAPTER 11

Sonny wiggled in his chair, uncomfortable with the stares Katrin and Coleen aimed at him. Their expressions were almost identical even though the two women looked very different. He could only describe it as icy empathy. *I should have braved the gnomes and gone drunken Christmas tree hunting.*

Flufflepuff curled in his lap, a warm weight of support.

Janine and several other Rocchi family members worked in the kitchen, cooking a feast for the evening. Apparently, this week was about eating and sharing time with family—a family he wasn't really a part of.

"You work in a potion shop, huh?" Niels gave him a strained smile, then mouthed, *I'm so sorry.*

Sonny cleared his throat. "Yes. My mentor and I run the place."

"Your spelled spaghetti was good," Katrin said, mouth curving in a half smile.

Coleen winced, then shuddered. "Don't remind us

of that, Mom." Her gaze sharpened on Sonny. "Leo is the type to want to settle down, Sonny. You seem nice, but you two aren't mates. He's a bear shifter, and one day, his mate is going to show up. What will you do then?"

Turn them into a donut and flush them down the toilet. Wait, we are mates, so I don't have to worry about that. I think. Leo sure hadn't acted like they were mates.

He shook his head, trying to clear his thoughts. "That's between Leo and me."

"Is it though?" Katrin asked. "This is a family gathering and he invited you. Like Coleen said, you seem nice, but you aren't family. He shouldn't have brought you."

"Mom," Niels said, eyes shocked.

Flufflepuff poked her head over the table and hissed at Katrin.

Sonny blinked away tears, a hard knot forming in his stomach. He knew he wasn't family. No matter what Leo said, Sonny would never be his family. Maybe they were right. *Maybe we're not mates.*

Katrin gave Fluff a wary look. "I promise I'm not trying to be cruel, Sonny, but I know my son and his heart gets involved too quickly. Please understand. He's not for you."

"Damn it, Katrin," Janine said, stomping to the table. "I leave for five minutes and you break Sonny's heart. You don't know what you're talking about."

"I'm just being honest." Katrin winced. "You're far better than that awful Dillion, but you're a witch. You can't be Leo's mate. He certainly doesn't act all that protective or possessive of you, and you haven't been claimed."

Flufflepuff hopped on the table, hair standing on end, and hissed loudly.

Sonny covered his mouth, stifling his cry. She was right. *We're not mates. We can't be. What was I thinking? Why didn't I listen to Aaron?*

Janine held her hands up, worn face full of anger. "Enough, Katrin. You truly don't know a thing about Leo and Sonny's relationship." She pulled Sonny out of the chair. "Grab your cat, sweetheart. I can see those thoughts churning in your head. We need some air."

Katrin sat up straight, face red. "Janine, I'm just—"

"I said enough," Janine interrupted. "Keep your mouth shut for five fucking minutes."

Coleen glared at Flufflepuff when the cat swatted at her. "Grandma—"

"You too, Coleen." Janine shook her head. "I've never been more disappointed in my family than I am right now."

Niels squeaked and covered his mouth while Katrin and Coleen looked devastated at Janine's words.

Sonny wiped his eyes and picked up Flufflepuff, burying his face against her fur. "Settle down, girl. I know the truth can hurt."

Janine pulled him toward the backdoor. "Sonny and I are going to milk the cows."

Sonny told his heart to stop thumping so loudly and his eyes to quit leaking, but it didn't work. *I love him. I love Leo and want us to be mates. Goddess, why does this have to hurt so much?*

Janine grabbed their coats and pushed him through the door. "Oh, sweetheart, that look on your face just about kills me. I'm glad Leo isn't here right now. He'd have some choice words for his mama, and those words would be hard to forgive."

She tugged her coat on and wrapped his around his shoulders, making him slip his arms through one at a time before zipping it up to cover Flufflepuff. Then she pulled a warm knitted cap over his head and down to cover his ears. After donning her own mittens, she patted his cheeks. "Things will work out like they should as soon as Leo gets back, sweetheart. Let's go milk the girls. They're good producers so we milk them three times a day."

He followed behind her, mind muddled and vision still blurry from the damn eye leakage. He was happy that he'd worn his low-heeled boots since he'd have to hike through snow and cow poo.

The walkway leading to the large red barn was paved and clear of snow. Janine noticed his surprise and shook her head. "Have you ever milked a cow, Sonny?"

Sonny wrinkled his nose. "No. We get our milk in jugs like the Goddess intended."

Janine chuckled. "City witches. What can you do with them?"

They slipped into the warmth of the barn and Sonny looked around, surprised at the cleanliness. He didn't see cow poo anywhere. He let Flufflepuff out and his familiar went to sniff around.

"Our girls are over here." Janine walked toward the back. "Now, the first thing you need to do is say hello."

Sonny followed behind her and stared into the first cow's liquid eyes. The brown lady was in a stall filled with straw and looked fairly standard for a cow.

"Moo," she lowed deeply.

"Moo to you too, ma'am," Sonny said, nodding.

Janine smiled. "Since you and Daisy get along so well, I'll let you milk her."

She went on to explain the milking process, but Sonny only heard about half of what she said. He had found the cow poo. There was a big pile of it in the corner of Daisy's stall.

Janine patted his shoulder, then pushed him through Daisy's gate. "Let me know if you need any help. Remember to use lube."

He yelped. *What the hell am I doing?* "I don't know her that well!"

Janine laughed. "For your hands. Dear lord, I'm going to have fun with you, sweetie." She tossed him a pair of latex gloves. "Just wear gloves if you don't want to lube up. Holler if you need me."

She went to the next stall, and Sonny slipped his gloves on while contemplating Daisy. "Your boobies, my darling Daisy, are too far down. Normally, I would kneel, but don't think I've forgotten that huge pile of poo I spotted earlier."

He waved a hand and mumbled a simple incantation to levitate Daisy. *Why kneel when Daisy can float?*

"Moo!" Daisy's legs started kicking in panic as she rose in the air.

"Whoa, calm down, Daisy." Sonny tried to steady her, but she was too scared.

Daisy kicked out, striking him in the shoulder, and he fell back, butt landing in the huge pile of cow poo. Sonny's lip trembled and he squeezed his eyes closed. He could feel the warmth of the shit seeping through his favorite jeans. A whine escaped him, then like a dam breaking, his tears came, hard and ugly.

"Moo!" Daisy kicked and kicked, floating through the air like a demented bird.

"What the hell?" Janine stared at him, then at Daisy. "What did you do, Sonny?"

Daisy quieted down as she floated around the barn, brown eyes darting around with interest.

"My cow's flying," Janine said in wonder.

Sonny covered his face and cried harder. *I'm a fucked-up failure of a witch. No wonder fate wouldn't give me Leo for a mate. He's not my honey bear.*

The barn door opened and Katrin and Coleen walked in, bringing a cold blast of air with them.

"We're sorry, Sonny," Katrin said. "We didn't mean to upset... Daisy's floating. What the hell?"

The two women watched as the cow floated out of the barn and into the yard.

Janine rolled her eyes. "Don't just stand there. Catch Daisy before she floats to the neighbor's house. You know they've been trying to buy her."

Katrin and Coleen ran outside, and Janine knelt

beside him. "Sweetheart, I know you're upset, but I need your help with Daisy."

He mumbled something, not even sure what he was trying to say, and took her hand, letting her help him stand.

She spun him around and winced when she saw his backside. "You're a mess, but we'll get you clean." She put an arm around his shoulders and walked him out of the barn.

Katrin and Coleen each had one of Daisy's hoofs. Other family members were trying to help too, but Daisy kept floating higher.

Niels saw him and winced. "I can smell you from here."

"Damn it, witch," Coleen said, scowling. "Look at the mess you've made. Why couldn't Leo have found a nice bear?"

An image of Leo with someone else popped into his head and anger shot through him. Sonny's eyes narrowed and he growled, snapping his fingers. Coleen's head shimmered for a moment before shifting into a pecan pie. The other Rocchi family members scrambled back in surprise.

Katrin kept a hand on Daisy's hoof, but her feet started to rise from the ground. "Coleen, keep your mouth shut. Oh shit, you don't have a mouth."

"Sonny." Janine looked horrified. "I hate pecan pie. Why didn't you give her a pumpkin pie head instead?"

Several vehicles pulled into the driveway, and in seconds, the rest of the Rocchi family was filling the yard. Sonny sniffed and wiped his nose, eyeing the

Christmas trees. *I see they were successful. Good for fucking them.*

Rosemarie went to her sister and studied Coleen. "I like this new look of yours."

"She deserved it," Niels said, nodding. "It does suit her well, don't you think?"

Leo looked at Katrin, Daisy, and Coleen. "Sunshine, what did they do?"

Sonny's eyes watered again and the tears were back. Leo took one look at him and opened his arms. Sonny ran to him and sobbed against his chest.

"I'm not family," he said, pushing his head into Leo's jacket and mumbling. "I hate your sister and cows stink."

"Okay," Leo said simply. "Do you want to go home? We can grab our bags and be on the road in five minutes."

"Leo, it's Christmas," Jesse said, grabbing at Katrin as she floated higher. "You can't just leave your family."

Leo's growl rumbled deep in his chest. "Sonny *is* my family."

Thorwald pushed through the crowd and waved his hand in front of his nose. "Bro, your witch seriously smells, but I'd still do him."

Sonny leaned back when Leo began to shift. He watched in amazement as Leo growled, eyes glaring at his brother.

"My mate!" Leo yelled, voice deepened by the shift. Then it was done and he was a large brown bear chasing his brother around the yard with death in his eyes.

"Oh dear," Janine said, laughter in her voice. "Ronald, will you keep Leo from killing Thor for talking about his mate? We'll deal with Daisy."

Ronald grinned and shifted, clothes scattering around him. A few of the other Rocchi family members did the same, then set off to intercept Leo.

"Mate?" Katrin was completely off the ground now, but Jesse had her about the waist. "Really? You're Leo's mate? Of course, you are. That makes perfect sense. Oh, Sonny, I'm so sorry."

Sonny blinked, Leo's words settling inside him like a warm slice of apple pie. *My mate! They were mates. Leo was his and nothing could keep them apart. Nothing.*

A grin slowly moved across his face, and he started dancing in place, hips wiggling and arms waving in the air. "We're mates, we're mates, we're mates!"

Janine laughed. "Sonny, calm down."

Sonny pulled her into his dance and they whirled around the yard, feet hampered by the snow. "Leo and I are mates, Janine!"

"Yes, you are." She shook her head and laughed at him.

"Uh, Sonny? Help, please." Jesse's feet were barely touching the ground.

Sonny waved his hand toward them and practically sang the spell to lower Daisy. "Uh, sorry about that, Janine."

"No problem, sweetie. Daisy needed an adventure." She glared at one of the stray Rocchi men. "Alfred, help Katrin and Niels get Daisy back into the barn. I can't believe you all just stood there while Katrin practically floated away."

Sonny continued dancing until Leo stood in front of him, completely naked. "Honey bear, cover the goods. We don't need them getting frostbite and falling off."

Leo growled and picked him up, throwing him over his shoulder. "Mate."

Sonny squealed. "Is this really happening? My laid-back honey bear is really going all shifter on me?"

"I'm claiming you," Leo said, voice deep and rumbly. "You're mine, sunshine."

CHAPTER 12

*L*eo's head was full of a roar of emotion. Thorwald had *looked* at his mate. His mom and sister had *hurt* his mate. A foul smell cleared his thoughts a bit. His poor mate was covered in shit. Covered in it! It was too much.

Distantly, he could admit that he was grateful his grandpa and uncles had kept him from maiming Thor, but it would have been nice to at least get in a swipe or two.

He carried Sonny straight to the bathroom down the hall from their room. His mate didn't like being dirty, and Leo needed him naked.

Sonny slid down the front of his body, making Leo's already hard dick that much harder. "You know we're mates now?"

Leo wanted to bite himself. "I've known since I met you."

Sonny's dreamy expression disappeared, and Leo

worried he'd have a pecan pie head soon. "You knew? Why the hell didn't you say anything?"

Leo knelt on the floor and started tugging Sonny's shoes off. "I didn't know how you'd respond to it since you're not a shifter, and honestly, I wanted you to love me for me, not because we're mates."

Sonny glared at him. "I knew we were mates. Witches can scry to find out. I knew right after Halloween."

Leo paused in pulling Sonny's pants down. "Really?"

Sonny sighed and cupped his face, looking down at him. "Honey bear, it's a good thing I love you or your head would be a pecan pie right now."

"You love me?" Leo felt his bear settle happily inside him, chasing away the last of the fogginess.

Sonny stepped out of his pants and bent to kiss him. "I really, really do."

"Can I claim you? Please?" Leo's bear grumbled that this was a very good idea.

"Finally." Sonny's head fell back and he stared at the ceiling. "Goddess help me, he finally wants to claim me."

"Uh, I've wanted to claim you for as long as I've known you." Leo stood up and turned the shower on. He almost fell in when Sonny pounced on him.

Sonny kissed him, wrapping his arms and legs around Leo's body and practically climbing him.

Leo started to suggest they shower, then go back to their room, but he couldn't wait another second. His bear wanted his mate.

Leo pulled Sonny up and into the shower, hands

bracing his ass as they ground against one another. He buried his head against Sonny's neck, breathing his mate's scent in and letting it go straight to his dick.

After a few moments of stretching Sonny's ass and lubing up, Leo finally slid into his mate, relishing the familiar feeling of Sonny around his dick. He moved slowly, suddenly able to tolerate the wait. He had his sunshine in his arms now, so everything didn't seem so urgent.

His teeth scraped along Sonny's neck. "I love you, Sonny." Leo could hear his bear in the low rumble of his voice. "I will love you forever." He sank his teeth into Leo's neck, drawing blood and ensuring his mark would remain on his mate for the rest of their lives.

Sonny yelled and came, splattering come between them. He clung to Leo and moved his hips furiously, milking Leo's dick as he came, filling his mate. His teeth stayed locked in place as his dick hardened again.

"Leo?" Sonny leaned back and gave him a dazed look. "Already?"

"Shoulda done this in the bedroom," Leo mumbled around his bite. He braced Sonny against the shower wall and pounded into him. His bear would make sure their mate knew they belonged together.

A FEW HOURS LATER, LEO CARRIED A FRESHLY SHOWERED and almost naked Sonny down the hall to their room. Of course, his siblings and cousins lined the hallway, hollering and cheering.

"About time, bro," Thorwald said, grinning.

Leo growled at him, unhappy his jerk of a brother was seeing parts of Sonny that he shouldn't.

"Hey now, no harm meant," Thorwald said, holding up his hands. "You know why I was pushing you."

Leo stopped and tilted his head. "Huh?"

"It was clear to Thor and me that he was your mate," Burkhart said, grinning. He held Flufflepuff in his arms. "Thor was just trying to push you into admitting it to us."

Leo narrowed his eyes. "I hate you both."

Sonny yawned and smacked his chest. "Carry me to the room, mate. I'm feeling the urge to make honey cakes."

The noise in the hall grew almost unbearable. "Sunshine, we're bears. You know what saying that does to us."

Sonny settled his head on Leo's shoulder and watched him, eyes full of emotion. "I know. I want to do something special for you and your family."

"We're your family too," Coleen said, head no longer a pecan pie. "I'm sorry, Sonny. I was way out of line and should have kept my mouth shut. Even if you weren't Leo's mate, it was clear to everyone that he loves you."

Sonny gave her a shy smile. "Really?"

Rosemarie elbowed their sister out of the way. "Really. Now make us honey cakes."

An hour and one miracle later, Sonny and Leo had somehow managed to get the kitchen to themselves. Leo sat at the table and watched his mate work his magic. A tiny potion bottle stood next to the mixing bowl.

"That's more honey than you normally use," Leo said, leaning back in his chair and folding his hands over his stomach. Flufflepuff curled up against his neck, purring.

"I'm making a different recipe," Sonny said. "Myrtle taught it to me. It's a Russian honey cake recipe and it will have to be chilled overnight. We can serve them for winter solstice." He looked over his shoulder, winking. "The trick to this one is to add more butter. Then some cinnamon for protection, and, of course, wildflower honey for happiness. Finally, just a dab of this calming potion to make everyone feel good and relaxed."

Leo smiled, perfectly content to watch his mate spell his obnoxious family.

~

THE NEXT EVENING, EVERYONE GATHERED IN FRONT OF the fireplace. They would wait until Christmas Day to exchange most of their gifts, but Sonny was a witch and today was winter solstice.

Leo grinned as he looked at all the presents piled on the coffee table. Each person had gone and gotten something for Sonny to welcome him into the family. *Maybe they aren't so bad.*

Sonny pressed his hands to his cheeks. He sat in the recliner of honor and looked particularly beautiful in his silver and blue sparkly dress. "This is too much. You all didn't have to do all of this."

"We did," Katrin said, nodding firmly. "We weren't kind to you, Sonny. This is our way of apologizing and welcoming you to the family."

"You said gift giving is a way to show your loved ones that you care," Coleen said. "This is our way of saying we care. You make Leo happy and we love the dumbass, so we're thankful."

"Gee, thanks," Leo said, arching a brow.

"Mine first," Burkhart said, reaching under his chair. "I can't wait until Christmas. I found this at a truck stop on the way up here." He reached inside a box and pulled out a tiny black kitten. "He was just sitting in the dumpster. Can you believe that? He's been staying in my room." He handed him to Sonny. "He's a black cat, so he goes with a witch, right?"

"That is a rotten stereotype and you should be flogged." Sonny took the kitten and cuddled him close. "He's such a cute little baby. Flufflepuff, what do you think?"

Flufflepuff jumped into Sonny's lap and sniffed the kitten before licking his face.

"She approves," Leo said, smiling. He nodded at Burkhart. *He really is my favorite.*

Leo watched his family hand over their presents for Sonny. This was what he had wanted from the beginning. He loved his family and all their obnoxiousness. He wanted Sonny to have that same loyalty and unconditional love.

He smiled when the kitten launched itself to Sonny's shoulder. Sonny rolled his eyes and scratched

Flufflepuff's head. "You're already teaching him bad habits, Fluff."

Leo laughed along with everyone else, but his focus stayed on Sonny, not the cats. *I will love him forever.*

PART III
CANDY HEARTS AND A
WITCH'S RING

Holiday Omegas: Book Three

*S*onny snuggled deeper into Leo's embrace. He knew he needed to get up, but there was no better place to be than in his mate's arms.

He rubbed the warm mating scar on his neck. Heat tingled through him, and he breathed in Leo's familiar scent. Ever since the day they'd officially mated, they had been going at it like bunnies.

Sonny wrinkled his nose. *Eww, now I'm thinking of bunny sex. Hmm, I wonder if Aaron and Gemma do it in their rabbit forms?*

"What are you thinking about, sunshine?" Leo's grumbly voice sent a shiver down Sonny's back.

"You don't want to know." Sonny ran his fingers through Leo's thick chest hair. "Today's going to be busy at the garage, right?"

Leo groaned and rolled over, taking Sonny with him. "Yes. Everyone is booked solid for the next two weeks. We have two more hours to snuggle before we have to get up."

Sonny nipped at Leo's shoulder. "I'm getting up early. I want to make your family something special for lunch to help you all get through the day."

Leo's growl rumbled in his chest. "You need rest too. Lay back down, and don't worry about it."

Sonny sat up and smacked Leo's chest. "I *want* to do it, honey bear. Don't try bossing me around."

Leo chuckled. "I know better."

A soft scrambling noise drew their attention. Ravenpaw climbed onto the bed and went straight to Sonny's still warm pillow. The kitten that Sonny had gotten for Winter Solstice had grown quite a bit over the past month, but he was still very much a kitten.

Leo rolled over and smiled as they watched the kitten curl into a little black ball of fluff and settle down to sleep. "I'll get up too. I like watching you cook."

Sonny smiled widely. "I'll pack you extra honey cakes too."

Leo sat up and raised his arms into the air. "Yes!"

Sonny laughed as he slid out of bed. "Shower with me."

"Even better." Leo hurried out of the bed and tripped on the covers, stumbling a bit before he straightened up. "You didn't see that."

"I saw it all, and you're lucky I didn't have my phone turned on." Sonny chuckled and started brushing his teeth. His ass was still a little sore from the night before, and his body ached in all the best ways.

Leo went to the second sink and reached for his toothbrush. Since the quick renovation, their master bathroom was much larger. Looking at all his makeup boxes and beauty products, Sonny conceded that it was probably a good thing.

"Is Tilisha working today?" Leo asked, yawning.

"Yes. Thank goddess." Myrtle had finally recognized that they needed another witch at the potion shop. Sonny hated to admit it, but Myrtle was getting older, and she didn't really need to keep working full-time hours. "Stupid, fucking Valentine's Day is coming in a few weeks and people are already placing orders."

Leo grinned. "I really don't get why you hate the holiday so much."

Sonny scowled. "It's a senseless, commercialized holiday that tries to force people to participate." He slammed his tooth brush down. "Plus, it completely overshadows Imbolc."

Imbolc was probably one of Sonny's favorite holidays. It was meant to celebrate the goddess as the maiden – spiritually whole *without* a partner. The holiday was a fresh breath of air in the dead of winter and was about accepting and loving yourself. *Then stupid non-witches had to turn it into a holiday that celebrates being part of a couple.*

Leo snorted. "Sure thing, sunshine." He wrapped his arms around Sonny and nuzzled his neck. "I love you."

Sonny's irritation disappeared. "I love you too."

Leo herded him into the shower, and Sonny almost immediately slipped to his knees.

Leo chuckled. "You don't have to –"

Sonny sucked one of Leo's heavy balls into his mouth, and his mate's words turned into a groan.

Sonny stroked Leo's hard length, then swirled his tongue around the head. *Better than buttercream frosting.*

Leo braced his hands against the side of the shower, and Sonny changed his angle, taking more of Leo's dick into his mouth.

Sonny felt Leo's muscles tense and prepared to drink down Leo's release, but the bear shifter surprised him.

Leo growled and pulled his dick out of Sonny's mouth. "Want inside you." He helped Sonny stand, then spun him around, pinning him to the shower wall.

His mate's hands cupped Sonny's ass almost reverently. Leo lowered to his knees and placed several tiny, gentle bites on each cheek.

He slid his fingers through Sonny's crease and found his hole. Using lube, he slowly stretched Sonny's ass, one finger, then two, then three.

Sonny moaned and pushed back, riding Leo's fingers.

After a moment, Leo stood and nibbled the back of Sonny's neck. "Love you." He bit down hard and thrust into Sonny's ass.

Sonny cried out and arched his back as Leo pounded into him. Leo gripped Sonny's hips and lifted him half off his feet, angling his body so Leo's dick hit just the right spot.

"Fuck, fuck, fuck." Sonny panted, trying not to come so quickly. It didn't work. Leo's dick hit his prostate again, and he came all over the shower wall.

Leo didn't last much longer. He grunted and held Sonny still as he came, filling Sonny's ass.

He slowly lowered Sonny to his feet and wrapped his arms around him. "Shower sex is the best."

"You say bed sex is the best when we're in bed." Sonny snickered. "Then, there's couch sex, counter sex, floor sex, stairs sex, and window sex. Don't be so fickle, honey bear."

Leo sighed. "I love all the sex."

Sonny turned in his arms and snuggled against him as the warm water fell over them. His bear gave the best hugs in the world. "We should shower, huh?"

Leo laughed. "Yeah. I'm glad we did the larger shower with the renovation. I don't know what I would do if I couldn't shower with you."

They finished quickly and dried each other off.

Sonny looked through his closet, rubbing his chin. *First, I need to shave. Now, what to wear today.* He settled on a pair of distressed skinny jeans and a warm green V-neck sweater.

Now shoes. He moved to his shoe closet and looked it over. "Remember when you said we didn't need a shoe closet?"

Leo snorted. "I was a fool."

"Yes, you were."

Sonny's mate was already dressed in jeans and a long-sleeved t-shirt. He sat in a chair next to the balcony doors with Flufflepuff, Sonny's familiar, on his lap, purring loudly. *Hussy cat.*

Sonny grabbed a pair of brown, heeled ankle booties, stopping to nuzzle the kitten. *Never say no to heels.*

He scooped up Ravenpaw on his way to the

bathroom. "Remember when I had a familiar that loved me more than anything?"

Leo laughed. "Fluff still loves you. By the way, she's coming to work with me today."

Sonny stuck his tongue out at them, then shut the bathroom door. After shaving and fixing his short brown hair, Sonny dressed. He clasped on a pretty bronze Celtic knot bracelet that Leo's grandma Janine had given him for Winter Solstice.

He tucked Ravenpaw in the pouch pocket of his sweater and left the bedroom. The renovation had taken a full month but should have taken a lot longer. Myrtle had spent most of her time over that month bossing the construction workers around to *make sure they got it right.*

Fortunately, the construction workers had ignored her for the most part. Personally, Sonny thought they worked so quickly so they could get away from the old woman.

Sonny grinned. He couldn't complain, really. He now had a two-story apartment with a large master bedroom, three small bedrooms, and a private spelling kitchen. *The two balconies will come in handy when it isn't so damn cold outside.*

He went downstairs and found Leo making pancakes. The bear wasn't the best cook, but he could make pancakes with the best of them.

Leo looked up and grinned. "Can you share the kitchen?"

"I'll try." Sonny bit his lip to hide his smile. "It's so cold outside. How does chili sound for lunch?"

"Delicious."

Sonny hummed and gathered his ingredients. "Chili powder to enhance the spell, cumin and salt to purify the garage from all negativity, bay leaves for protection, oregano for happiness and luck, garlic to give a health boost, and a little cayenne pepper for extra strength to get you through the day."

Leo eyed him. "I thought oregano went into our special love spaghetti."

Sonny laughed. "It does, but every herb and spice has multiple uses. It's the intention of the witch that gives them their *job* in the spell."

"Okay." Leo shifted his feet. "I just don't want Mom and Dad to have quickies all day. It's traumatizing."

Sonny smiled slyly as he started chopping an onion. "Katrin requested a pot of spaghetti for her anniversary next month."

Leo shuddered. "Please don't tell me things like that."

"You're ridiculous," Sonny said, exasperated. "Sex is an established and natural part of their relationship. Katrin and Jesse have very active sex drives, kinda like us."

Leo shook his head and covered his ears. "No, no, no, no."

"You're going to burn the pancakes." Sonny tried to hide his amusement but didn't think he was too successful.

"I love you and hate you right now." Leo shook his head and turned back to the pancakes. "My love for pancakes will save breakfast."

Sonny laughed and started heating the olive oil. "Changing the topic now because I really do love you too. February through May is especially busy at the shop with Ostara and Beltane." *Please, please ask me why.*

"Okay." Leo shrugged. "Let me know if you have to work late, and I'll bring you dinner. Is Miles going to start training at the shop?"

Sonny held back a disappointed sigh. "Yeah. He'll be training there with me starting next week."

Leo gave him an oblivious smile. "I'll have to bring you both dinner."

CHAPTER 14

*B*y mid-morning, Sonny wished he would have kept some of the chili for himself. The shop had been busy as soon as the doors opened. Tilisha was glued to the register. Her dark eyes kept shooting him desperate looks, but he couldn't find a second to help her.

"You're sure this fairy sugar milk will work?" Mrs. O'Dell asked doubtfully.

Sonny smiled widely, wishing he could throw something. He was so tired of people already. "Yes. All you need to do is pour it into a bowl. Set an oatmeal cookie drizzled with honey next to it, then light a white candle. You know the incantation."

"It's just that I haven't seen a fairy in a long time, not since I was girl." Mrs. O'Dell gave him a rueful look. "I don't mean to be difficult, but it gets awful lonely now that the kids are all out of the house. I'm hoping to entice a fairy to come stay with me. Bert already made a little fairy house for one just in case."

Sonny's smile felt more genuine this time. "I understand. Fairies are pretty illusive though. Usually, they'll come and bless your home while you aren't looking, then leave with their cookie and sugar milk."

"Well, I can always hope." Mrs. O'Dell patted his arm. "You're busy today, so I'll leave you be." She watched Ravenpaw for a moment. The kitten was curled on Sonny's shoulder. "I thought your familiar was a white fluffy cat."

"Flufflepuff is currently with my mate," Sonny said dryly. "Ravenpaw here is filling in for her while she's gone."

Mrs. O'Dell's eyes brightened. "Oh my! A mate? Who's the lucky witch?"

Sonny flushed. "He's a bear shifter actually. Leo Rocchi."

The older woman's mouth fell open. "A bear? That's preposterous. Witches mate witches. Are you sure you're mated? Did you do a proper Ostara scrying?"

Sonny tapped down his anger. *Myrtle won't like it if you turn a customer's head into a pecan pie.* "We haven't spent an Ostara together. We began dating in October."

Mrs. O'Dell shook her head and tsked. "Your father is one of the best hedge witches this side of town. He'll do your Ostara scrying, won't he? I wouldn't go around saying you're mated without at least doing the scrying. Then what about your Beltane binding? Shifters don't know our traditions. Would this bear even be willing to put in all the work to get to a handfasting?"

Myrtle bustled over with a box of potions. "Shirley,

all that nonsense is just formality. You know that. Anyway, Sonny did his own scrying and doesn't need that useless bag of beetle eggs to tell him anything. Our catbear already claimed him too. Look at his neck. Obviously, Leo likes the mark to stay fresh."

Sonny slapped a hand over his mating mark. "Myrtle!"

Mrs. O'Dell gave them an uncertain smile. "I better go check out."

After she had left, Myrtle glared at him. "Something's been itching you, Sonny. What's wrong?"

Sonny rolled his eyes and took the box of potions. "Now isn't the time for a heart to heart."

Myrtle watched him in silence as he started shelving the potions. "You're happy with Leo, aren't you?"

He spun around, hand holding Ravenpaw in place. "Yes! He's literally my favorite person in the world. Even more favorite than you and Aaron."

Myrtle chuckled, face softening. "Now I know you love the man. What's the problem then?"

Sonny turned back to the shelf. "Ostara is in March."

"Yes?"

"Shifters don't do scryings, bindings, or handfastings. Once you're claimed, you're considered married. We filled out paperwork and everything." Sonny smiled softly when he thought about how Leo's grandma had already had the paperwork ready for them.

"That doesn't mean you can't have a proper Ostara scrying and a Beltane binding before your handfasting." Myrtle scowled and started helping him with the potions. "I know you've been planning your handfasting since you were six or seven. Hell, you made Aaron promise to do the bunny boogie at it. What's the problem?"

Sonny let a breath out slowly. "Leo hasn't mentioned it. At all. I don't think he'll want to do a handfasting, little less all the rest of it."

Myrtle blinked. "He hasn't mentioned it at all? Don't you two talk about anything important or do the two of you just fuck?"

Sonny winced. "We talk about stuff."

"Stuff." Myrtle shook her head. "Thank the goddess I'm past the young and dumb stage of life."

"What's that supposed to mean?"

"It means you should just tell Leo about our traditions. How else is he supposed to figure it out? Ostara's in March, damn it. If you miss it, you'll have to wait until next year for the scrying and binding. Then you'll have to wait another year for the actual handfasting. The timing is important, butternut. Witches take their time for a reason, and clearly, you and Leo need that time to pull you heads out of your asses. Besides, do you really want to go two years without being fully mated to your bear?"

Sonny shook his head. "I can't just blurt that out. I don't want to make Leo feel like he *has* to do something to keep me. You said it yourself. All those things are just formalities. I should be happy with what I have."

Myrtle sighed. "They're traditions, Sonny. They aren't necessary, but they sure are nice."

Sonny swallowed back his tears. "I can live without a handfasting."

Myrtle shook her head and walked away, muttering under her breath.

By the afternoon, the shop had only slowed down a little bit. "The afterwork crowd will be here in a couple of hours." Sonny texted Miles's mother. "Tilisha do you want a break? I'll have my apprentice meet me here for our lesson. I don't want to leave you alone."

Tilisha's smile was grateful. "That would be wonderful. I'll pick you up a coffee too. Your baked goods are all already gone. Do you want me to pick anything up while I'm out?"

"I have ingredients in the back, and Miles will help me get some things going for the late crowd." Sonny patted her shoulder. "Go get some fresh air."

They both looked outside at the snow and ice.

Tilisha arched a brow. "Yes, I'll enjoy that."

Sonny pushed back his exhaustion and smiled for the next customer. *Maybe I should have taken those two hours of sleep instead of getting up early this morning.* Ravenpaw was already napping on the back of one of the comfortable chairs by the front windows. *Smart kitten.*

An hour later, Tilisha was back from her break, and Miles was shrugging out of his winter coat.

Sonny's apprentice grinned, eyes bright with happiness. "Sonny, guess what?"

Sonny smiled softly. "You've decided to becoming a

traveling musician and are going to start practicing the harmonica?"

Miles rolled his eyes. "No. If I became a traveling musician, I would learn how to play the banjo."

Sonny nodded, keeping his expression grave. "Of course. So sorry."

Miles smiled again. "I'm in love. Her name is Tilly, and she's in my class."

Sonny gasped, hand to his chest. "When is the Ostara scrying?"

Miles laughed. "I can't get handfasted yet. Mom won't let me." A shy look crossed his face. "She's an owl shifter."

Sonny steered Miles toward the back, waving at Tilisha as they passed her. "That's neat. Owls are beautiful creatures. Does she like Cookie?"

Miles's familiar was currently curled up in the seat of Ravenpaw's armchair, yawning.

Miles nodded enthusiastically. "She does. I need your help with something."

"Anything."

"Valentine's Day is coming up."

Sonny hissed. "You dare mention that horrid commercialized holiday in my presence?"

Miles snickered. "I dare. I want to make her some spelled candy hearts."

Sonny groaned. "I don't know if I can participate in anything related to that dreadful day."

"Please?" Miles's eyes widened, and he gave Sonny a beseeching look. "For me?"

"Cookie taught you that look, didn't he?"

"Maybe." Miles fluttered his lashes. "Please, Sonny? You're my only hope."

Sonny chuckled. "Fine. What kind of spell are we talking about here? Love spells are out."

Miles shuddered. "No love spells. I told you I was done with those. I just want to make her happy and maybe give her a boost for school. She's struggling with a book report."

Sonny tapped his chin. "Okay. Peppermint, vanilla, and sugar. Peppermint is my favorite herb, you know."

Miles grinned. "I know. It's good for boosting happiness and optimism. You use it a lot."

Sonny nodded, feeling an abnormal amount of pride for his apprentice. "Yes. It's also good for focused studying and writing."

"Really?" Miles's looked happy. "What about vanilla? It's good for happiness and energy."

"It's also good for your self-esteem." Sonny nodded and started gathering ingredients. "Imbolc is next week, you know. That's far more important than stupid Valentine's Day. Giving your Tilly a boost of self-confidence is much better than roses or chocolates."

Miles nodded, eyes watching Sonny's every move. "You're right. Then there's sugar. It attracts."

"Yes." Sonny eyed Miles curiously. "What do you want to attract for her?"

Miles's face twisted in concentration as he thought. "Joy. I want to give her joy."

Sonny's eyes watered. *Damn, I love this kid.* "You

know what? Let's make a bunch of candy hearts. We should sell them in the store, and I want to give some to Leo."

Miles's eyes widened. "My idea is good?"

"Very good."

CHAPTER 15

*L*eo carried Flufflepuff tucked into his jacket and the pot of chili tucked under his arm as he walked from his truck to Rocchi's Garage. "It's too damn cold for you, sweetheart."

"Meow." Flufflepuff curled against him, sounding pitiful. *Do cats need sweaters? I need to ask Sonny. I bet Grandma would make Fluff some sweaters.*

The door to the garage had barely closed behind him when his sister Coleen ran toward him, waving a magazine over her head. "Leo, you've fucked up. Big time!"

"Huh?" Leo set the pot of chili down and unzipped his jacket to let Flufflepuff hop onto the front desk. "Did I screw up the SUV from yesterday? It was running well when I gave it back to Charlie."

Coleen smacked him with the magazine. "No. You've fucked up with Sonny."

Leo's eyes widened, and he froze. Sonny was his

C.W. GRAY

world, and the thought that he had messed something up made his gut churn. "What are you talking about?"

"I was reading *The Modern Witch*." Coleen waved the magazine in front of him. "I was such a jerk last month, so I've been trying to learn more about witches so I can connect with Sonny like Rosemarie and Niels do."

Leo smiled softly. "That's sweet, Coleen. You know he really does like you. I just think you two don't have a lot in common."

She flushed and looked away. "Yeah, I know, but that doesn't mean we can't be good friends. Anyway, so I was reading the magazine, and there's all this stuff about handfasting. Apparently, it's a *big* deal in witch society. There's like a whole formal process, and it involves Ostara and Beltane. That's not that far away, and I know you haven't even asked him yet. There's a lot to do, and you're dragging your ass, Leo. It's kinda like a wedding, but all witchy, so you need to think of a venue, reception, who's going to officiate, the wedding party, and clothes –"

Leo shook his head. "What are you talking about? Sonny and I are mated. It's done."

She gave him a disbelieving look. "He's not a shifter, Leo. Claiming your mate works for shifter society, but witches are different."

Witches are different. Leo felt a little lightheaded and sat down behind the desk. "Oh, fuck. I didn't even think about that. What do witches do for their mates? He said he did a scrying after we met to confirm I was his. Is that not all?"

Coleen shook her head, looking panicked. "No, not

even a little. They're all about rituals and ceremonies. Hasn't he said anything?"

Leo felt his bottom lip tremble. "No. Do you think... Do you think he doesn't *want* to be mated to me? Otherwise he would have said something, right?"

Coleen hugged him. "As confident and sassy as Sonny appears, he's still really self-conscious. You didn't see his face when Mom and I told him you weren't his mate at Winter Solstice. He was devastated, Leo. Maybe he's afraid to bother you with all the stuff that goes with handfasting. There's a scrying and something called a binding."

Flufflepuff jumped into his lap, and Leo stroked her ears and head. "Did you know about this, Fluff?"

"Meow." Sonny's familiar watched him with sad eyes.

"You should have said something." Leo sighed. "I have to fix this."

Coleen let him go and opened her magazine. "Okay, so the first step in courting a witch is to show your understanding and appreciation of their family traditions and heritage."

"Well, I've fucked that up already." Leo made a face. "I didn't even think about what Sonny expected from a mating."

"Imbolc is coming up." Coleen grabbed a notepad and started writing. "You need to show him you appreciate the tradition."

Leo groaned. "I laughed at him this morning when he was talking about Imbolc and some other holiday. He was cursing Valentine's Day."

C.W. GRAY

Coleen winced. "Nice work, little brother. Imbolc is February first, and they have all types of traditions that go with it. We'll talk to Myrtle and figure out a game plan for you." She looked up from her notepad. "What about his heritage? Witch heritage is supposed to be significant. What witch family does he descend from?"

"His last name is Thornton?" Leo gave her a puzzled look. "Is that what you mean?"

Coleen rolled her eyes. "No, Leo. A lot of witches can trace their bloodline back to one of the powerful council families."

He eyed Coleen suspiciously. "You read all that in a magazine?"

She made a face. "No. I've been researching. I told you that."

Leo's shoulders slumped. "I don't know anything more than his last name and that he's estranged from his blood family who live a few blocks from here. Myrtle and Aaron are his family."

She propped her hands on her hips. "Well, you need to find out before Imbolc so that you can show your respect. After that, you need to prepare for Ostara. That's when the scrying happens. I don't know what it's for, but that's when it occurs."

Leo straightened up and nodded. "I'll do whatever I have to."

Coleen waved him away. "Go to your station. I'll keep taking notes, and we'll talk at lunch."

Leo stood and set Flufflpuff on the floor. He picked Coleen up and hugged her tightly. "You're the best, Coleen. Thank you for helping."

Coleen smacked his chest. "It's what family does. You might not want to thank me after I talk to Mom about this."

"Do you have to?" Leo was a little ashamed of the whine in his voice.

Coleen arched a brow. "We're going to need all the help we can get. I don't think you understand the severity of the situation."

BY THE TIME LUNCH ARRIVED, ALL LEO COULD THINK about was what a shitty mate he was. He had known Sonny was his for months, but he hadn't thought to look up witch mating traditions. What kind of mate did that? *A bad mate,* he thought sourly. *A very bad mate.*

"Come on, Leo." His brother Burkhart thumped him on the back. "We need to figure this shitstorm of yours out."

Leo blinked and finished closing the door to his station. "Huh?"

"Coleen spread the word." Niels, the youngest of them, scooped up Flufflepuff from where she napped on a stack of tires. "We're having a family meeting over lunch."

Burkhart pushed his back, and Leo stumbled toward the breakroom where everyone was gathered.

Though they loved their clients, one rule that Leo's mom and dad stood firm on was lunch time at the Rocchi Garage. No matter how many appointments there were that day, the garage closed for an hour for lunch.

Katrin Rocchi stood next to the refrigerator, tapping her foot impatiently. She held a bowl of Sonny's chili in her hand. "Hurry, hurry, boys. We have a lot to do."

Leo grabbed Flufflepuff's herring snack and set it on the table before getting a bowl of chili for himself.

"I can't believe we all missed how important handfastings are to witches." Niels settled Fluff on her spot at the table and went for his own lunch.

Jesse, Leo's dad, sighed. "To be fair, there aren't too many interspecies matings. If Sonny were mated to another witch, they would already know about witch customs and traditions."

Leo growled. "Sonny is mine."

Flufflepuff looked up from her lunch and hissed toward Jesse.

Jesse snorted. "Settle down, you two. I'm not saying Sonny doesn't belong with you, Leo."

"You're wrong anyway." Rosemarie made a face at their dad. "There *are* plenty of interspecies matings, but most people don't like them, so they either don't mate or keep a low profile. Think about the Dawson family."

Rosemarie was the only one that didn't growl that time. Seven growling bears and a hissing cat made for a tense atmosphere.

Sally Dawson and Leo's mom had been friends for years. Leo and his brothers and sisters had spent many a day at the Dawson house while growing up. Niels had been good friends with Sally's youngest daughter and Burk with her oldest daughter. She had always welcomed Leo with a hug and a smile when she saw him.

Then, two weeks ago, Sally had shown up at the garage to tell them all that they weren't welcome around her family anymore. The way she had looked at Leo made him shudder even now. She thought he was some kind of monster.

"Assholes," Thorwald said, scowling.

Rosemarie rolled her eyes at them and held her hands up. "I'm not saying the Dawsons were right about anything. I'm just saying a lot of people would agree with them. You were Sally's friend for a long time, Mom, and she still cut you off because Leo didn't mate a bear."

"I think we see what you mean, Rosie." Jesse frowned. "How do we fix this?"

Coleen cleared her throat and held her notebook up. "I have answers, but it's going to take all of us to pull this off." She looked at Leo. "You need to start by asking Sonny about Imbolc. Experience the holiday with him. Talk about his family's heritage and all that shit."

Thorwald winced. "But don't call it shit."

Leo arched a brow and sniffed. "I know that much, Thor."

The blond smirked and shrugged. "You're the one that didn't know about handfasting."

"Like you did?" Leo asked, disbelieving.

"Boys." Katrin's hard voice made them both hush

and sit up straight. She nodded to Coleen. "Go on, sweetie."

Coleen grinned. "Mom and Dad need to meet with Myrtle and start planning the handfasting for the day after Beltane. It really is a lot of work. I think witches take a full year to plan it, but –"

"Not happening." Leo shook his head. "I'm not waiting a year to witchy claim my mate."

"Witchy claim?" Niels snickered.

Coleen glared at him. "As I was saying before I was so rudely interrupted, *but* you probably don't want to wait that long."

"Hell no, he doesn't want to wait that long now that he knows something's missing," Burkhart said, looking horrified. "No shifter would. It'll be hard enough to wait until May."

Leo nodded in agreement. "My bear is content we're mated, but my head is all screwed up. We need to fix this fast."

"We'll go see Myrtle tonight." Jesse looked grim. "It needs to be perfect, so the sooner we start planning the better."

"Good." Coleen pointed at Burkhart and Thorwald. "You two need to start working on our family. You know they're always down for a good party, but they need to know it's happening. The handfasting will be May Day, so they need to start clearing their calendars. Mom and Dad will let you know where it will be. I've got a list here of appropriate gifts for a handfasting."

"On it." Thorwald grabbed her note and started

reading over it. "Um, why are there diapers on here?" He eyed Leo. "You have something you want to tell us?"

Leo blinked. "Huh?"

Coleen sighed. "Leo, the months before Beltane are going to be Sonny's most fertile time. Your mating is so new, so he's going to be all over you. From what I understand, it's milder than a shifter omega's heat, but it lasts from Ostara to just after Beltane. Plus, every witch that attends the handfasting is going to be giving you all fertility blessings. A baby is going to happen. That's almost a given. A lot of witch families fully expect a baby to be conceived the night of the handfasting, so it's customary for handfasting gifts to take this into account."

Leo leaned back, face slack. *A baby? Already?*

Coleen ignored him and looked at Niels and Rosemarie. "There are a lot of supplies they'll need for the activities for Imbolc and Ostara. You two are in charge of gathering everything. I'm sure if you need help finding something, Myrtle can point you in the right direction." She handed Rosemarie a huge stack of papers.

"Holy shit." Rosemarie started looking through them. "I don't know what most of this stuff is."

Coleen gave her a hard look. "Figure it out. We need to get this right." She turned to Leo. "You and I are going to go over everything you need to do and what you need to know. The internet can only tell us so much, so we need to meet with some witches."

Leo shook his head, trying to clear the fog. *A baby witch with Sonny's eyes. What kind of familiar will they have? They can spend time at the farm with Grandpa and Grandma like I did as a kid.*

"Leo!" Coleen snapped her fingers in front of his face. "We need to start working on the rings, the ribbons, and getting the family blessing. There's no time for daydreaming."

CHAPTER 16

At the end of the day, Leo sat in his truck outside of the garage. He looked at the number Coleen had given him.

"Flufflepuff, I don't know if this is a good idea." He looked at the passenger seat. Sonny's familiar watched him sadly. "I don't have much choice, do I? Sonny doesn't talk about them, but he still calls them once a month. He'll want them at the handfasting."

"Meow." Flufflepuff didn't look too impressed with his reasoning.

He dialed the number before he lost his courage.

"Thornton residence," a brisk voice answered.

"Um, hi. I was hoping to talk to Travis or Cynthia." Leo swallowed hard. "Please."

"I'm Cynthia." Sonny's mom sounded curious.

"My name is Leo, and I'm mated to Sonny."

"Sonny." Cynthia's voice went flat. "Unless he has decided to become *normal*, we don't want anything to do with him. Just because he's an omega doesn't mean he's not a man. Has he finally decided to act like one?"

Leo growled. "Watch your fucking tone. Sonny is a beautiful person who deserves respect and love."

"I don't have time for this." She ended the call.

"Fuck her." Leo gritted his teeth and threw the phone onto the floorboard. "Fluff, we know who Sonny's family is. Aaron and Myrtle are a hell of a lot better than that asshole. We don't need them."

"Meow." Flufflepuff nodded and raised one of her paws for a high five.

Leo tapped her paw with a finger. "We need to talk to Myrtle."

He made the quick drive to the apartment complex and parked his truck. Myrtle owned the complex, but for some reason, she was perfectly content to live in a small ground-floor apartment instead of taking one of the bigger units.

Leo knocked on her door.

Myrtle answered. The older woman wore yoga pants and a long-sleeved t-shirt with the words *village witch* running across the front. Her ferret familiar, Toddlebug, stretched across her shoulders.

She scowled. "What do you want, catbear? It's my meditation time."

"I have questions. Important ones." Leo pushed past her and made a path to the couch through her cluttered apartment. He set Flufflepuff on one of the plump pillows, then spun around. "Have you spoken to Mom and Dad yet?"

Myrtle rolled her eyes. "Goddess help me, they just

called ten minutes ago. I was taking a shit. I'll call them back."

"We don't have time, Myrtle!" Leo ran his hands through his hair. "Beltane is four months away! I don't know anything about planning a handfasting. Then, tonight, I called his mom and she's horrible. She was so rude, and I was rude back. I don't know what to do."

Myrtle blinked. "Okay. Sit down, catbear. You need to relax. I have some special brownies. Do you need one?"

"I don't want your pot brownies, Myrtle." Leo fell onto the couch. "I need your help to fix this."

Myrtle snorted. "Alright then. First thing first, you got your info wrong. The tradition is to propose with a ring at Ostara, then have a ribbon binding on Beltane. Then, you have to wait a year and a day to have the handfasting."

Leo gave her a horrified look. "A year? I can't wait a year to finish mating Sonny. My bear and I want him now."

Myrtle sighed and picked up a box of tissues. She tossed it at him, hitting him right in the forehead. "Stop being so impatient, damn it. Young folks are so annoying. Now, you wait a year and a day for a reason. It's supposed to show your true commitment and understanding of one another. You two clearly need it. Talk more, catbear. Fuck less. I feel like you both need the words tattooed on your foreheads."

"Witches wait a whole year to fully mate?" Leo hadn't lasted two months in claiming Sonny.

Myrtle arched a brow. "Sometimes they wait longer.

For us, mating is more than bodies and hearts. It's about the merging of souls and minds. You need to take the year to learn Sonny. He needs the time to learn you too."

Leo bit his lip. "I have to?"

She gave him a hard look. "Do you want Sonny to be happy?"

"Yes." He sighed. "I'd wait a fucking lifetime if it's what he wanted." He brightened at a sudden realization. "So, I'm not behind on mating Sonny?"

Myrtle rolled her eyes. "Oh, you are way behind. You need to plan the Ostara scrying and your proposal. I'll do the scrying, of course, but the proposal is all on you. It needs to be special, Leo. Then there's the Beltane binding. It's not a handfasting, but it's still important." She narrowed her eyes. "My Sonny deserves the best. You had better get to showing that you care."

Leo nodded, utterly determined to be the best mate ever. "I'll start with Imbolc."

CHAPTER 17

*S*onny woke slowly. He had been so tired from work yesterday, and Leo had been strangely quiet over dinner. They had both made an early day of it.

He yawned and wiggled back against Leo's familiar body, then frowned. *Something doesn't feel right.*

Sonny lifted the covers. His mate's big hand was cupping his abdomen. That's not what Leo usually cupped.

Leo nuzzled the back of Sonny's neck, distracting him. "You're taking it easy today, right?"

Sonny hummed under his breath and arched his hips back. Leo's hard length pressed against the crease in Sonny's ass. "Yeah. The shop is only open half a day, and Myrtle and Tilisha are working." *Today is a free day with my honey bear, and I know how I want to spend it.*

Leo pulled away and swung his legs over the bed, and Sonny fell back, huffing with annoyance.

Leo leaned over and kissed his forehead before he

started grabbing clothes. "Well, I have some errands to run this morning. Do you want to meet with Aaron and Gemma for lunch?"

Sonny narrowed his eyes. "What about lazy morning sex? We *always* have lazy morning sex when we both have off from work."

Leo almost whimpered. "I don't have time, sunshine. I'm so sorry."

Sonny pushed the covers aside and got up. "Fine. I'll just hang out with Flufflepuff and Ravenpaw today."

Flufflepuff currently slept in the smaller cat tree in the corner of the room. Ravenpaw was lying on his back inside the tree, batting at a feather hanging from the higher level.

"I thought I'd take –" Leo started, then stopped when Sonny glared at him. "Never mind. I'll start breakfast. Pancakes okay?"

Sonny sighed softly, irritation softening. "That's perfect."

Leo ran to the bathroom and shut the door.

"I don't even get shower sex," Sonny grumbled and went to the closet. "Today is definitely a cute sweater and leggings kind of day."

He pulled out a pair of gray leggings, a long white tunic, and an oversized soft pink and gray cardigan. He grabbed his knee-high, heeled black boots and set them aside. He picked up a heavy vintage bear charm with a long chain and a pretty clasp bracelet with pink rosebuds on it. Both were gifts from Janine.

Leo yawned when he came out from the bathroom

and gave Sonny a long kiss before leaving the bedroom with Ravenpaw on his shoulder.

Sonny tapped his chin. "Flufflepuff, something's off with Leo." He looked at his familiar. "Do you know what it is?"

"Meow." Flufflepuff watched him with deep, wise green eyes.

Calm settled into his mind and tension drained from his shoulders. "You're right, Fluff. I just need to trust my mate. He loves me and will tell me what's going on with time."

Sonny took his time with his makeup and hair, then dressed. By the time he made it downstairs, Leo was setting the plates on the table.

Sonny snapped his fingers to light the brown candle at the center of the table. *Blessings on our home, our pets, and the apartment grounds.*

Leo hummed happily. "I like your candles. They're all over, and I know they each mean something." He cleared his throat. "What does this one mean?"

Sonny blinked for a moment, surprised. Leo hadn't asked about Sonny's craft before. "Uh, brown candles are used for stability and blessings of the home, animals, and the earth."

"How do you light them like that? I kinda thought all your magic went into baked goods, but you've done a few other spells too."

Sonny eyed him. *Something is definitely off.* "It's about transferring energy. My energy is best channeled through baking, yes, but I can still do other things too. I'm just better when I use my kitchen witch skills."

Leo nodded and drizzled honey over his pancakes. "Myrtle trained you, right? You said your mom was a kitchen witch and your dad a hedge witch. Did they teach you a lot too?"

Sonny took a bite of bacon and chewed thoughtfully. *What's going on, honey bear?* "My mom taught me as much as Myrtle when I was a child. When I started being more"—he gestured to his makeup and outfit—"she stopped taking an interest in my training. Dad taught me some of the basics of hedge witchery before my affinity testing."

Leo watched him carefully. "Affinity testing? That happens real young, right?"

"Yeah, around the age of eight or nine. The young witch goes to the local council and is tested for their affinity and magical strength. There's this whole celebration and everything." Sonny smiled and propped his chin on his fist. "My parents threw a party and the whole family came. I had fun that day." *It was the last time his parents had ever looked proud of him.*

"The whole family?" Leo arched a brow. "Were there more than Thorntons there?"

That's an odd question. Sonny eyed Leo. "Yeah. Dad is descended from the Blackwood family and Mom the Whitmore family. Both are known for their, uh, fruitfulness. Let's just say twins and triplets are the norm."

Leo paled and started swaying in his chair.

Sonny jumped up. "Are you okay?" He braced Leo up and felt his head. "You don't have a fever. Do you think you caught something at the garage? Hold on and

146

I'll get you one of Myrtle's tonics. They boost your immune system."

"I'm alright." Leo hugged him, then pushed him away. "Eat your breakfast."

Sonny sat down and tried to control his worry. "Are you sure?"

"Yeah." Leo gave him a shaky smile. "So, do you have siblings? I thought you were an only child."

Sonny winced. "I am. Dad and Mom kind of went against family tradition and only had one kid. They wanted to take on more apprentices instead of breed enough to fill an army like the rest of the family."

"What about you?" Leo asked, eyes wide and almost glowing gold.

Sonny grinned. "I want a kid or two one day. We've never had this conversation, have we? It seems important, and we missed it. What about you?"

"Yeah." Leo shook his head furiously. "I want lots of kids with you."

Sonny bit his lip to hide a smile. He liked the way Leo said that. *Kids with you.*

Leo licked his lips. "Uh, so I was thinking that we could celebrate Imbolc together."

Sonny made a face. "I don't do Valentine's Day."

Leo shook his head. "No, I said Imbolc. We could do some of the traditions together like make wreathes and a besom and maybe bake some stuff. Mom and Dad want to have a dinner to celebrate, and we can walk around the park and look for signs of spring."

Sonny opened his mouth, then closed it. Finally, he found his voice. "You want to do that with me?"

"Yeah. Isn't that what you do for Imbolc?"

Sonny nodded. "Yes, but I thought it would just be me and Myrtle this year. Sometimes Aaron does stuff with us, but with Gemma carrying a kit, he'll be busy."

Leo put another pancake on Sonny's plate. "I want to know more about your traditions and heritage, Sonny. We're mates, and you're important to me. I wish I would have asked you questions months ago."

Sonny reached out and squeezed Leo's hand. "Thank you." He made a face. "We can do something for Valentine's Day if you want. I guess if you're willing to celebrate my holidays, I can celebrate a stupid, commercialized farce of a holiday."

Leo grinned. "Your willingness to compromise astounds me."

CHAPTER 18

*A*few hours later, Sonny sat in a coffee shop
with Rosemarie. They watched a pretty, dark-
skinned barista work.

Sonny sipped his latte, then sighed. "You know she's
your mate, so why won't you even talk to her, Rosie?"

Rosemarie shushed him, then smiled nervously
when Kate looked over at them, eyebrows raised.

As soon as Kate looked away, Rosemarie pinched
Sonny's arm. "Shifter hearing, dumbass."

"Oops." Sonny tried to sound sorry, but he had a
feeling she didn't believe him. "Answer my question."

A couple of weeks ago, Rosemarie had brought him
a lock of Kate's hair so he could do a scrying for her.
Rosemarie's nose didn't work like other shifters', so she
needed confirmation that Kate was her mate. It just so
happened that Kate *was* Rosemarie's mate.

Rosemarie leaned forward and whispered directly
against his ear. "She has to know she's my mate, but she
hasn't even asked me out."

149

Sonny sat back and gave her a disbelieving look. "Seriously? You're pining away because she hasn't asked you out yet? What are you, a Victorian maiden worried about filling your dance card? Go talk to her, Rosie."

Kate snorted and shot them an amused look.

"Sonny," Rosemarie practically hissed. "Don't embarrass me."

"You're doing that all on your own." He sipped his coffee. "Communication is important to any relationship. You need to be clear about what you want. Maybe she's waiting on you to ask her out."

Rosemarie glared at him as she stood. "Alright already. I'm going up there."

Sonny struggled not to laugh as she stomped toward the bar.

Kate set the espresso she had just made down and walked from behind the counter. She met Rosemarie halfway.

The two women started at each other a moment, Rosemarie looking constipated and Kate looking on the verge of laughter. Finally, Kate snorted, then leaned forward and kissed Rosemarie.

Sonny quickly snapped a picture and texted it to Leo and the rest of his family. "That's my little Rosie," he said, sniffling. "I told you communication was... Shit. Communication *is* important to a mating."

His shoulders slumped. He wanted a handfasting and all the trappings that went with it. There was no way around that. He wanted one, and he hadn't said anything to Leo about it. Sonny had just waited and hoped that his honey bear would read his mind. *It's time to stop passively waiting for what I want.*

Sonny stood up quickly and grabbed his shoulder bag. Flufflepuff poked her head out. "Meow."

"Hush," he whispered. "No pets or companions allowed in here, Fluff."

"Meow."

"Yes, I know I said I was going to spend time with you, then stuffed you in a bag. I'm a bad witch and I'm sorry." He gave Rosemarie and Kate one last smile, then left the coffeeshop.

An hour later, he sat in a small, warm Italian restaurant with Aaron, his best friend. They were a little early, so both Gemma and Leo weren't there yet.

Sonny refreshed his lip gloss. "Rosemarie texted me. She's on her way to Kate's apartment now."

Aaron grinned and pumped his fist in the air. "Finally! What was taking them so long?"

Sonny made a face. "Kate recognized Rosemarie as her mate right off, but Rosemarie couldn't tell for sure. She *thought* Kate was her mate but wanted to make sure. They both thought the other must not want them since they didn't jump each other as soon as they sensed they were mates. Silly shifters."

Aaron stuck his tongue out at Sonny. "Silly witch."

Sonny put his lip gloss back in his bag. "I am silly, Aaron. I want a handfasting."

Aaron looked confused, prominent front teeth chewing his bottom lip. "Okay? Does Leo not want one? I can't see him denying you anything you want. That bear worships the ground you walk on."

Sonny groaned. "I haven't told him. I was so happy when he claimed me because I knew it was important to shifter culture, and I've been trying so hard not to think about a handfasting because I know you shifters don't do anything like that for a mating. It just doesn't feel right not to honor my traditions, but I didn't say anything to him."

Aaron snickered. "You're a dumbass."

"I am." Sonny propped his head on his chin and slid an anchovy into his bag. A fluffy white paw grabbed it. "I should have just told him about it. Now, I'm going to have to broach the topic and hope he'll at least consider it. Witches grow up knowing how involved mating is. What if it's too much?"

"He'll do it for you." Aaron's shoulders slumped. "I'm going to have to dance the bunny boogie, aren't I?"

"The bunny boogie?" Leo's deep voice came from behind them, and they both jumped. "What's that?"

Sonny smiled softly when Leo helped Gemma into her seat. Aaron's mate was about seven months pregnant and moving quite a bit slower. *My gentleman bear.*

Leo unzipped his coat and slipped Ravenpaw down and into Sonny's bag. *My covert gentleman bear.* Sonny's mind wandered as he envisioned Leo as a spy. *No one would suspect him.*

"Sonny?" Leo's voice was full of amusement. "What's the bunny boogie?"

"Yeah." Gemma grabbed a breadstick. "I haven't heard of it."

Aaron whimpered. "It's nothing at all."

Sonny gave them a dreamy look. "It all started in preschool."

"Please, Sonny," Aaron begged him. "Please don't do this."

Gemma looked between them, curiosity growing. "Oh, please *do* tell us whatever my darling mate is hiding."

"It was my first day of preschool, and I didn't know anyone." Sonny sighed dramatically. "The other kids were ignoring me, so I was upset. I wanted to go home and play with my stuffies."

Leo got a faraway look in his eyes. "I bet you were a cute kid."

"He was all big eyes and floppy brown hair," Aaron said, smiling. He gave Sonny a fond look. "He had one of his teddy bears with him and looked so alone."

"After no one sat with me at snack time, I got upset and started to cry." Sonny pressed a hand to his heart. "There I was, all alone and devastated."

Gemma snickered. "Oh, the drama!"

"Then, my knight came to my rescue." Sonny blew a kiss to Aaron. "A young rabbit shifter gave me a hug and asked me why I was crying."

"He wouldn't answer." Aaron flushed. "He just kept giving me sad looks and hugging me."

Sonny nodded. "I couldn't help it. So, to dry my tears, my beloved knight showed me his secret. He shifted into his rabbit form."

Gemma exchanged a confused look with Leo. "That was a secret?" she asked.

"No." Sonny shook his head and closed his eyes, picturing that day. "He stood up on his hind feet and started dancing the bunny boogie. He raised his paws and shook them right, then left. Then he shimmied and turned. Finally, his shook his cute little butt for a solid minute. Then he did it over and over again."

Leo grinned, then started laughing.

Gemma shook with her giggles. "Oh damn, Aaron. Did you really do that?"

Aaron buried his face in his arms. "It made him stop crying. He laughed and clapped instead."

Tears streamed down her face as she laughed. "I have to see it. I really, really have to see it."

"He danced it for me every time I was sad for years," Sonny said, smiling at Aaron. "You'll always be my bunny knight."

Aaron shot him a dirty look. "We finally agreed to retire the dance when we were in middle school."

Gemma finally composed herself. "No. I need to see it."

Aaron gave Leo a sly look. "I agreed to dance it at Sonny's handfasting."

"Handfasting?" Gemma looked thoughtful. "Wait! I forgot. Witches do a handfasting ceremony when they mate, right?"

Sonny drew in a sharp breath and looked at Leo.

Leo looked panicked, and Sonny's stomach knotted. *Maybe he does know about handfasting. Maybe he just doesn't want to do it.*

Leo shook his head and stuffed a breadstick into Gemma's mouth. "We can't talk about that until Ostara."

Sonny sat still, processing Leo's words as Aaron quickly changed the topic. *He knows! Leo knows he's supposed to propose at Ostara.*

Sonny's grin was slow and wide, and his eyes watered. He knew he looked like a love-sick idiot, but he didn't care. "I love you, Leopold Rocchi."

Gemma and Aaron made kissy faces, but Sonny didn't mind at all. Leo was looking back at him, eyes full of an emotion Sonny was very familiar with – love. "Love you too, Sonny Thornton."

LATER THAT NIGHT, SONNY WATCHED FROM THE LOWER balcony as Leo, in shifted form, sat on his butt in the snow. The large brown bear's front paws clutched his back paws, and he rocked back and forth as he waited for Miles to get there.

Flufflepuff curled around Ravenpaw, keeping the kitten warm. She licked his head and settled hers on top of his.

"Look at him," Sonny whispered, burrowing into his warm coat. "My mate is a pancake king and a covert gentleman bear." *He takes care of me and respects me, likes my friends, worships my body, and loves me just the way I am.* "I'm one lucky witch."

Miles reached Leo, and Sonny could see his apprentice waving his hands as he talked animatedly.

"I want my handfasting to be in the park here. I'm thinking a large honey cake, some oatmeal cookies, as many flowers as possible, and I want a May pole." Sonny practically shook with happiness. "I'm getting my handfasting."

CHAPTER 19

FEBRUARY 1ST, IMBOLC

*L*eo arched his hips, struggling not to come as Sonny rode his dick. His witch's hands were braced on Leo's chest, and their eyes were locked. Sonny's intense gaze made him shudder.

He flipped them and raised Sonny's hands above his head, pinning them to the mattress. Sonny whimpered, then clenched his ass around Leo's dick, making him groan.

Something had changed between them a week ago. It probably wouldn't have been noticeable if Leo hadn't been watching his mate closely as he prepared for Imbolc and Ostara. Sonny was happier.

Sonny chuckled warmly. "My mate." He leaned up and nibble Leo's bottom lip before kissing him.

Leo slowed his movements and angled his hips, focusing on driving Sonny wild. It didn't take long.

"Fuck," Sonny groaned, splattering cum between them.

Leo bit down on Sonny's mating mark, and his

witch shuddered again. Leo came hard, filling Sonny's ass.

A few moments passed as their breathing slowed. Leo nuzzled Sonny's neck and breathed in his familiar honey scent. *My witch, my mate.*

Sonny hummed and snuggled against him. "It feels strange not working the morning shift at the potion shop. It's Imbolc, so I know they're busy."

Leo hid his smile. Myrtle had been all too happy to give Sonny the day off. "We have plans."

Sonny blinked. "Huh? It's Wednesday. Don't you work?"

"Nope." Leo kissed his forehead. "I told you we were going to celebrate together."

Sonny bit his lip. "I thought you might have forgotten."

"I've made plans for us today and tomorrow." Leo groaned as he sat up. "We really should get up."

Sonny jumped out of bed and wiggled in place. "What are we doing today? Can't you feel the energy in the air? I love Imbolc; it's so refreshing! It's about self-care, the coming of spring, welcoming the sun, honoring our ancestors, and so much more."

Leo nodded, smiling. "I can't wait to share it with you. Now, to start, I thought we'd have a nice and relaxing morning. Why don't we light some of your candles to start purifying the house? Then, I'll run you a nice bath."

Sonny barely stifled his squeal. "You'll take it with me, right?"

Leo grinned, utterly charmed by his mate's happiness. "I'd love to."

"The crone goddess sleeps and the maiden goddess awakens!" Sonny wiggled his ass, closed his eyes, and snapped his fingers. The white candles around the room were lit. "White candles for peace, self-enlightenment, purity, cleansing, rest, and joy." He snapped his fingers again and all the black candles in the room lit up. "Black candles for protection and to banish all negativity." One more finger snap lit the red candles. "Red candles for energy, vigor, and passion."

Leo shivered at the last word, his dick already starting to harden again. *Damn, that's some potent magic.*

Sonny sang out an incantation, and the words summoned a small gust of air that ran around the room, stirring the curtains and bedclothes. It swept the bedroom door open and disappeared down the hall.

Flufflepuff purred loudly and ran around Sonny, tail in the air and a spring in her step.

Ravenpaw looked a little scared, so Leo scooped him up. "This is new to you and me, right, little fella?"

Sonny's eyes popped open. "I need to bake some bread. I'll get it started while you run our bath." He grinned and hugged Leo and Ravenpaw. "We're going to have so much fun today!"

Leo grinned as he watched Sonny and Flufflepuff run out the door. "I think I love Imbolc too, Rav."

He went to his nightstand and dug out his cheat notes. "Okay, so we need to light some frankincense incense and pour this purifying potion of Myrtle's in our bath."

Ravenpaw's tiny meow made Leo smile. They went to the large master bathroom and started running a hot bath in the claw foot tub. He added Myrtle's potion and lit the incense.

Sonny ran in, Flufflepuff in his arms. "The dough is rising. I'm making Italian white bean soup and Rosemary bread. Later tonight, I think I'll make some cinnamon bread too."

"Anything you want." Leo waved toward the bath. "You ready to relax? Do we need to do something to the bread first?"

Sonny wiggled, still naked from their earlier fun. "Nope." He sniffed. "That's frankincense. How did you know to burn it?"

Leo felt his cheeks flush. "Uh, looked some stuff up and talked with Myrtle. Let's relax, huh?"

They climbed in, and Sonny settled his back against Leo's chest. He sighed and sunk into the water. "This is going to be the best Imbolc ever. I can already tell."

Leo kissed the top of his head. "This year is going to be best year. What are our plans, sunshine?"

Sonny chuckled. "Are we setting our intentions, honey bear? How do you know we do that on Imbolc?"

"Myrtle said so." Leo leaned back. "We have the house the way we like it. What about the shop? Do you all need to expand any?"

"We need to hire more help. Myrtle's shop has gotten popular in the neighborhood, and Gertie's place a few blocks away closed down when she retired so we picked up her business too." Sonny rolled his head over Leo's shoulder. "I think I'd like to plant more this year and expand my baked goods in the shop. You know Tilisha is a hedge witch too, right? She can help Myrtle with the potions, and I can focus on my yummy spelled goods."

"I think you'll like that."

"What about you?" Sonny asked.

Leo leaned his head back and stared at the white ceiling. "I want to be a good mate."

"You're already the best mate." He leaned back and gave Leo an exasperated look. "What else?"

Leo smiled. "Since I met you, I've gotten more comfortable in my skin. My weight doesn't bother me, and I don't think about my gut."

Sonny scowled. "You're a beautiful man, Leo."

Leo felt a piece of himself settle. "I am. I want to keep being beautiful this year. I want to spend more time in my bear form too."

"Those are good intentions."

Leo smiled. "They are."

They stayed in the bath until the water got cold.

Leo took his time drying Sonny. "Now, there should be a surprise downstairs for you, and you want to start on that soup too, right?"

"Yeah, I'm hungry. We forgot breakfast."

Leo winced. "I'm sorry, sunshine. For once, food wasn't the first thing on my mind."

Sonny rolled his eyes. "It's okay, Leo. I was more interested in our bath. Now, what's my surprise?"

"Let's get dressed and we'll go see."

They dressed and went downstairs. Leo could hear them all before they were even halfway down.

Sonny's eyes lit up. "Is that Janine?"

"It's everyone," Leo said dryly, unsurprised that his grandma was the one Sonny focused on.

Gathered in the large living room were Leo's grandparents, parents, and siblings. Aaron and Gemma cuddled on the loveseat. Myrtle fed a treat to her Toddlebug, and Miles and Cookie played with Flufflepuff and Ravenpaw in front of the fire.

Candles were lit around the room, and the dining table and coffee table were both covered in flowers and straw. *Rosemarie and Niels did well.*

"What's everyone doing here?" Sonny asked, grinning.

"We're here to celebrate Imbolc with you, sweetie." Janine pulled Sonny away from Leo and hugged him. "Myrtle and Miles have told us all about it, and it's a wonderful holiday."

Sonny leaned back and looked around the room, eyes watering. "The whole family? Just for Imbolc?"

"It's one of your favorite holidays," Myrtle said, shaking her head. "As many as witch society has and you love this one."

"It's a good holiday." Miles looked up from where he was scratching Ravenpaw's belly. "It's worth celebrating well, Sonny."

Sonny squealed and hugged Janine, dancing her around the room.

Leo grinned. *Yeah. My mate is a lot damn happier.*

Rosemarie stood up. "Okay, we got a lot of flowers and straw here. Myrtle says we need to work on making wreaths for protection and prosperity. I want those blue flowers. They remind me of Kate's eyes."

Sonny stopped dancing and arched a brow. "She has brown eyes."

"I didn't say they remind me of her eyes." Rosemarie huffed. "They have anything brown here anyway."

Leo chuckled. "Let's make some wreaths."

"And a besom!" Miles jumped up. "Mom and I made our besom this morning. Come on, Sonny. I'll help you."

Sonny clapped. "Okay. First, let me put the soup on, then we'll get started."

CHAPTER 20

*L*eo stood up from where he sat on the floor and stretched his back. A freshly made besom, which was apparently a broom made from twigs, stood next to the door to sweep away the old and make way for the new. Each of his family members now had a wreath. Some, like his grandma's, were put together well, while others, specifically Thorwald's, looked ready to fall apart.

They had spent the past few hours talking and laughing while they worked. It had been really nice. Leo had to admit this was a lot better than Valentine's Day.

Aaron checked his phone, then nodded at Leo. *Sonny's next surprise is ready.*

Leo sniffed the air. "Is it lunch time? That soup smells really good."

Sonny jumped up from where he sat with Miles and Coleen. "Yes. Let's have lunch."

"Oh, you sit down, sweetie." Janine stood up. "Ronald and I will feed you kids."

Leo's grandpa laughed. "You're always volunteering me for work."

Janine winked at her husband. "It keeps you young."

Sonny surprised Leo with a hug. "Thank you for doing this, honey bear. I've never had so much fun."

Leo squeezed him tightly. "The day isn't over yet. I have to admit that Coleen helped me quite a bit."

Sonny looked surprised. "Really?"

"Yeah. She wants you to like her."

Sonny frowned. "I do like her." He looked around until he spotted Coleen talking with Miles. Ravenpaw sat on her shoulder. "Apparently, she needs more hugs from me."

Leo snickered when Sonny surprised Coleen with a hug.

"That's a good person you have there." Katrin wrapped her arms around his waist. "Myrtle stole his handfasting diary, and we've been looking it over. Did you know he's been planning his handfasting since he was a kid?"

Leo groaned, guilt filling him. "I'm a horrible mate."

"No, you're not." Katrin smacked his side. "Sonny could have told you about handfastings at any time, and absolutely no one is perfect, Leo. You're going to make mistakes. Sonny will make mistakes. The key is to not let them ruin you. You two need to talk more and fool around less."

"Mom." Leo's cheeks heated. "Why does everyone keep saying that?"

She snickered. "Because it's true. Let's eat lunch."

They ate their bread and soup and chatted for another hour. Aaron started bouncing in place, and Leo knew he needed to move this along or Sonny's best friend would.

"Can I have everyone's attention?" Leo stood. "Part of celebrating Imbolc is honoring the earth and our ancestors. If you all will follow me to the roof of the building, Aaron, Miles, and I have a surprise for Sonny and Myrtle."

Sonny gasped and clapped. "More surprises? You're raising the bar for Imbolc, Leo. Are you sure you want to do that?"

Myrtle gave him a curious look. "Sonny and me?"

"Yeah." Miles grabbed Myrtle's arm. "You're gonna love it, Myrtle."

Leo wrapped an arm around Sonny and went to the door. "I think you're going to like it, sunshine."

Thorwald picked up his wreath. "I'm taking Betty with me. I've never made something like this, and I think I have a real knack for it."

Burkhart snorted. "You named it?"

Thorwald growled when Niels snickered.

"Boys!" Katrin glared at them. "Behave."

They all took the stairs to the roof, and Leo unlocked the roof access door.

"How did you get that key?" Myrtle asked, eyeing him suspiciously.

Leo shrugged. "I stole it."

Myrtle chortled. "That's my catbear."

He opened the door and led them out into the cold

air. Myrtle and the apartment complex's manager always kept the roof access to each building locked up. Leo thought that was truly a shame since there was so much available space there.

Miles's mom and dad were already there. Trish and Raul were both garden witches and were grinning proudly. All along the edge of the roof, Aaron and Raul had built raised plant beds. In the center of the roof was a small glass greenhouse that Leo had helped Aaron put up.

Sonny and Myrtle stared around, eyes wide and mouths open. They didn't say anything for a long time.

"It's a community garden," Leo said nervously. "We talked to the manager, Myrtle. He gave the go ahead to put one on each apartment building."

"We've prepared the soil and blessed it," Trish said excitedly. "Sonny and Myrtle, all you need to do is decide what you want to grow, and we'll plant it. Everyone can help take care of it."

Raul waved to the greenhouse. "We have plants started in here too. Take a look."

Myrtle and Sonny peeked in the door.

"That looks like yarrow." Myrtle grinned. "I'm always running out of yarrow."

Sonny's lip trembled, and he turned to stare at Leo with wet eyes. "You remembered. I told you I wished I had a garden." Leo's arms were suddenly full of Sonny. "I can't believe you all did this."

"I had help." Leo closed his eyes and hugged Sonny tightly. "The Blackwood family has a lot of talented garden witches. They created a unique rose."

Sonny leaned back, smiling. "I know. The Blackwood rose."

"Trish has one starting in the greenhouse. Once it's ready to plant, we can put it next to the door to our building." Leo swallowed. "Grandma brought some clippings of some of her favorite flowers on the farm too."

Sonny cupped his cheek. "Are we honoring our ancestors, honey bear?"

Leo nodded. "That's part of Imbolc." He smiled at Myrtle. "Your sister Hester sent a bunch of plants for the greenhouse. She said they were all grown from your mother's clippings years ago. She said you have most of them already, but more never hurts, right?"

Myrtle sniffed and wiped her eyes. "You're a good one, catbear." She hugged Miles. "So are you, little witch. You and your parents knew, didn't you?"

Miles giggled and hugged Myrtle. "We wanted to do something nice for you and Sonny. Aaron helped too."

Aaron smirked. "I'm more than a dancing rabbit." He ignored the curious stares and Gemma and Sonny's laughs. "Now, isn't there a blessing that needs doing?"

Myrtle laughed. "Trish? Why don't you do the honors?"

Miles's mom smiled widely. "My pleasure." She closed her eyes and spoke an incantation, voice smooth and melodic.

Sonny leaned his head on Leo's shoulder, eyes closed. "We honor the earth that sustains us."

The dark soil in the flowerbeds swirled around like churning water, and Leo felt something tug at his pants leg. Ravenpaw crawled up to his shoulder, burrowing against his neck. *Feels strange to me too.*

A deep resonating calm filled him. Leo looked over the apartment complex grounds. The large park was bare from winter, but he could almost feel the grass, trees, shrubs, and flowers growing. He had a sudden urge to shift.

"Go ahead," Sonny whispered against his ear.

Leo handed Ravenpaw to him and tugged his clothes off quickly. The shift poured over him, and his body shimmered and twisted until he stood in his bear form.

He looked around. The rest of his family had done the same. A white rabbit and a brown rabbit hopped around Miles and Cookie. *Gemma and Aaron must have felt it too.*

"I love your bear, Leo. I think you're right. He needs to come out more." Sonny curled against Leo's furry side. "This was a perfect Imbolc."

Leo settled down and watched the woods dance, Sonny, Ravenpaw, and Flufflepuff curled up with him. They still had a nice big dinner to cook and time to spend with their family. Today was just step one in claiming Sonny's inner witch.

I'll get this right, sunshine.

CHAPTER 21

MARCH 19TH, THE DAY BEFORE OSTARA

*S*onny danced around the potion shop, restocking shelves. Ravenpaw clung to his shoulder, and Flufflepuff slept in one of the windowsills. For once, the shop was empty. Tomorrow was Ostara, and most witch families had a lot to do to prepare.

It was almost closing time, and Sonny couldn't wait for the afternoon to be over. He knew Leo had plans for them. *I can't wait!* The past two months had been amazing. Leo was even more attentive than he had been, and they had spent so much time talking.

Tilisha hummed a tune as she set a crate of potions next to him. "As busy as it gets, I still love this time of year. There's an energy in the air that thrums through the body."

Sonny grinned. "Spring is here, and everything's coming alive. Our rooftop garden can finally be planted. Did I show you the picture of my rose bush?"

Tilisha laughed. "Only a thousand times." She patted

his cheek. "You and Leo are so sweet. I take it you're more than ready for your Ostara scrying and proposal?"

Sonny spun around, enjoying the way his violet skirt twirled around him. "Yes! Myrtle stole my handfasting journal and let it slip that she's already planning the handfasting with Leo's parents."

Tilisha gave him a fond look. "You have a handfasting journal?"

"Since I was six." Sonny shook his ass and danced as he went back to shelving potions. "I don't know why I thought I would be okay without a handfasting. I'm an idiot."

Tilisha shook her head. "You're just young. You and Leo are still learning one another. Being mates isn't a sure ticket to an idyllic marriage. That first year of mine, I thought for sure I'd murder my Jerome. He was such a slob."

Sonny snickered. "I'm going to tell him you –"

The door opened, and Sonny felt all the blood drain from his face. Flufflepuff stood up, hair standing on end as she hissed.

Cynthia Thornton had aged well in the last ten years, but there were a few more lines around her eyes and silver threaded through her brown hair. Her normally full lips were pressed in a thin line.

His throat was suddenly desperately dry. *Today was not the day to wear my new dirndl skirt.* "Mother." He glanced at Tilisha. "Can you go check inventory in the back?"

Tilisha made a face and grabbed her phone, typing

out a message. "I'll give you ten minutes." She glared at Cynthia before she left the room.

Cynthia ignored her and kept eyes narrowed on Sonny. "Somerset, what's this I hear of you mating a shifter? Haven't you harmed our family enough? My father was beside himself when he heard. *Your* father is so ashamed that he refuses to leave the house. The goddess would not possibly grant you a shifter as a mate. You're being as ridiculous as you look."

Sonny stifled a whimper and looked at the floor. He hated that her words had the power to hurt so much. "We are mates, Mother. I did a scrying, and he sensed me right away. Shifters recognize their mate's scent."

"No." Cynthia crossed her arms and stepped farther into the shop. "You've gone too far. That creature called our house, Somerset. He told me to *watch my tone*."

Sonny looked up, eyes wide. "Leo called you?"

"He said something about mating you, but I didn't know he was a shifter." Cynthia closed her eyes and gave a long-suffering sigh. "This has gone on long enough. Since our reputation is already shattered beyond repair, I'll be talking to the Witches Council about you. They surely won't approve. You will show up and agree to any action they choose to take."

Sonny gave her a confused look. "It's not illegal for a witch to mate a shifter."

Cynthia snarled. "It will be by the time you explain how that horrid beast abused and mistreated you. The Council would have to take action then."

Anger filled him. "Are you serious? I can't believe

even you would suggest something like that. Leo is the kindest and gentlest person I've ever met."

"You will do as I say." Cynthia held her finger in the air, the point glowing with a fiery green light. Sonny was well aware of how much pain her zaps could cause.

Fuck it. Fuck her. Her poisonous energy zaps had kept him in line as a child, but he wasn't a child anymore. "Get the hell out of my shop."

Cynthia waved her finger, and a green bolt zipped toward him, hitting him in the shoulder. Familiar pain moved through him, but he did his best to ignore it until he heard Ravenpaw yowl in pain.

"Rav!" Sonny winced as he shifted his shoulder and pulled Ravenpaw from around his neck. He checked the kitten over. He had a little singed spot on his fuzzy butt. His big blue eyes were full of fear.

Flufflepuff growled and jumped toward Cynthia, claws extended. Sonny's mother raised a hand and spit out a quick incantation, effectively freezing Fluff in the air. Flufflepuff growled low, eyes promising retribution.

Cynthia gave him a disdainful look. "I will happily kill this useless familiar if you don't obey me."

She shot another zap toward him, and he clutched Ravenpaw to his chest and spun around, taking the shot to his back. *Damn, that hurts.*

"I am your mother, Somerset, and you will come with me right now. I've had enough."

Sonny turned back to his mother, growling. "You are no family of mine."

She rolled her eyes. "I truly wish that were the case."

173

He snapped his fingers and quickly muttered his favorite spell. His mother's head disappeared, and a pecan pie took its place. "That should shut you up for a moment."

Flufflepuff fell to the floor, landing on her feet. She hissed and swiped Cynthia's bare legs several times.

If she could have, Sonny knew she would be yelling. Cynthia tried to dodge the swipes and smack at Sonny's familiar at the same time.

Flufflepuff dodged a swat and bit down hard on Cynthia's calf before running to Sonny's side.

Tilisha came from the back and leaned on the front desk. "Well, that look is a real improvement Mrs. Thornton."

Cynthia ran toward her, fingers curled into claws. The counter stopped her, so she raised her hands to her head, feeling around.

Tilisha ignored his mother and narrowed her eyes on him. "Are you hurt?"

"Just a couple little zaps." Sonny wheezed slightly when he tried to shrug. "She singed Ravenpaw's butt."

Tilisha glared at Cynthia and reached below the counter, grabbing a potion. She slid it across the counter, and it crashed to the floor in front of Sonny's mother. "Oops."

A horrid stench spread out, saturating Cynthia's clothing and body.

Sonny raised his brows. "I didn't know we sold skunk butt potions anymore. Didn't Myrtle get in trouble when those teenagers used some on their teacher?"

SONNY AND LEO

Tilisha shrugged. "I like to keep one behind the counter just in case. You never know when it will come in handy."

The front door slammed open, and Myrtle rushed in. Her gray hair was a mess, and she was clearly dressed for gardening.

Sonny sulked. *She's been planting in the community garden without me!*

Myrtle wrinkled her nose and eyed Cynthia. "It stinks in here."

Sonny held Ravenpaw up with his good arm. His left shoulder was still in pain, and his lower back ached. "She singed my kitten's bottom."

"She hurt Sonny too." Tilisha moved to hover over him. "How's that shoulder?"

Myrtle growled and muttered a few words. Cynthia's body twisted and transformed into a cockroach with a pecan pie head. "You're a foul woman, Cynthia Thornton. Get the hell out of our shop."

Sonny's mom scuttled across the floor, running under the chair.

Myrle stumbled forward when the door pushed open again.

Leo ran inside, eyes glowing gold. His parents and siblings were behind him, all dressed in their work clothes and looking close to shifting. "Sonny, are you alright?"

Katrin looked around. "Where's the bitch?"

Aaron and Gemma pushed in next. Aaron was vibrating with anger, and Gemma glared around the

175

room. She was close to giving birth, so Sonny wasn't sure what the hell she thought she could do to help anyone.

Sonny gave Tilisha a look. "Did you have to text everyone?"

Tilisha nodded. "Yes." She scowled. "She hurt Sonny and zapped Ravenpaw's butt."

Leo rushed to his side. "You're hurt? Where? Oh, sunshine. I should have gotten here sooner."

"I'll be okay. It'll just ache for an hour or so." Sonny flushed when they all looked at him. Aaron gave him a sympathetic look. He knew every dirty detail of what Sonny had gone through with his parents.

"Why do you sound so sure, Sonny?" Myrtle gave him a hard look. "Has she zapped you before?"

"I know what you're thinking, but they didn't hurt me." Sonny shook his head. "Not really. Mother just likes to zap when I get mouthy. It's fine."

Leo growled and pulled him into his arms. His big body shook with emotion. Flufflepuff purred as she wound around their feet. Her purrs settled into Sonny's mind, comforting him. He felt some of the anger drain from Leo as well. *Best familiar ever.*

Aaron took Ravenpaw from Sonny. "You stay right there, Sonny. I'll take a look at this poor little guy's bottom."

Myrtle's eye twitched. "She zapped you went you got mouthy?"

Katrin narrowed her eyes. "Where. Is. She?"

Myrtle glared at the chair. "I handled her."

Katrin stomped her foot. "That's not fair."

Myrtle gave her a sly look. "Keep your panties on fuzzbutt. I'll let you at her. She could use a beating." She snapped her fingers, and Cynthia transformed, tipping over the chair she had been hiding under.

Her eyes were wild as they darted around the room, and her legs still bled from Flufflepuff's attack. "You attacked me! The Witches Council will hear of this."

Katrin growled and pushed Sonny's mom, pinning her against the wall and baring her suddenly very sharp teeth. "You don't harm what's mine, witch."

Leo's family, along with Myrtle and Gemma, gathered behind Katrin, expressions dark with anger.

Cynthia swallowed. "Somerset is my son, and I didn't harm him. It was just a little zap."

Katrin held up her hand, or well, paw. She was far too close to shifting. "This will just be a little tap."

Cynthia squeaked and closed her eyes.

Sonny sighed. "Katrin, don't hurt her. I don't want you to go to jail. Just toss her outside."

Katrin growled.

"Please?" Sonny almost laughed when she gave him a frustrated look. "I'm done with her, and I just want her out of here."

Coleen pushed Katrin aside and grabbed Cynthia by the throat. "Out you go. I suggest you think twice before coming near our Sonny again. Got it?"

Sonny leaned his head against Leo's chest. "Katrin and Coleen are badass."

"They're the bosses. We just do as we're told." Leo stroked a hand up and down Sonny's back. "I'm sorry I

C.W. GRAY

called your mother. She wouldn't have bothered you if I hadn't."

"No, she heard I mated a shifter." Sonny sniffed deeply, Leo's scent soothing him. "I wanted her and my dad at the handfasting. I don't know why, but I've always pictured them there. I guess I held out hope they would want me again."

"Sunshine." Leo's voice was full of anguish. "I don't think they'll come, especially not now."

Sonny chuckled when he saw his mother running away from the shop. "I don't care anymore." He was amazed at the surety he felt. "It's time to let them go along with all the pain they bring. I have a family right here."

He would always carry a hole in his heart of his parents' making, but it was steadily filling up with another family. A much better family.

"Damn right you do." Aaron smoothed his hand over Sonny's head. "You're loved."

"Is Ravenpaw alright?" Sonny sniffled and looked for his kitten.

"His butt is uninjured. His fur was singed, and he's scared." Aaron handed him the kitten, and Sonny snuggled Ravenpaw.

Leo leaned back and eyed him. "Wait. How do you know about the handfasting plans?"

"So," Gemma said slowly, interrupting them. "Now that the nasty person is gone, I have a little problem."

Aaron's head whipped around. "Gem?"

She winced. "My water just broke."

CHAPTER 22

*T*welve exhausting hours later, Gemma and Aaron had a baby rabbit shifter named Wendy, and Sonny had serious baby jealousy.

"I think I should just keep her." Sonny rocked the bundled baby slowly. "Look at that sweet face."

"She's all wrinkly and red." Aaron grinned down at his newborn daughter. "Look what I made, Sonny."

"You?" Gemma scowled from the hospital bed.

Aaron waved her comment away. "We get to watch her grow up and live life. What do you think she'll be like?"

Sonny bumped his friend's shoulder with his own. "I think she'll have all kinds of adventures. She has her own personal witch. Imagine what her and I can get up to."

Gemma groaned. "Don't corrupt her."

Sonny gasped and gave Gemma a hurt look. All he could picture was his mother's look of disgust at his outfit the day before.

Gemma's brow wrinkled. "Why are you...." Realization came. "Oh, Sonny. I didn't mean you'd have any kind of influence over her gender. That's all on her. We love Wendy and will celebrate with her as she discovers who she is, no matter what she decides. Just like we love you."

Sonny's lip trembled, and Aaron tapped Sonny's chin, getting his attention. Sonny's friend wiggled his nose, and Sonny laughed, his hurt fading away. "Okay. Sorry about that. I guess I'm still a little raw."

Gemma leaned her head back against her pillow, looking far too beautiful for a woman who had just given birth. "I can imagine. You've had a hard afternoon. Wait. That was yesterday, right? I can't believe you stayed with us this whole time after all that drama. I have to admit, it was nice to have your hand to hold when Aaron passed out."

Aaron rolled his eyes. "I forgot to eat lunch. That's all."

Sonny snickered. "Sure, it is."

Aaron smirked and changed the topic. "It's Ostara, Sonny."

Sonny smiled slowly. "You know this is the perfect way for it to begin, right? Wendy is our little spring gift from the goddess to show us the cold and dark of winter is gone. You all will go back home to your nest soon."

Aaron hugged him, then went to kiss Gemma. "We did good, honey."

Gemma's eyes watered. "We really did. Fuck, I really

want my nest. Why did we have to come to the hospital again?"

"Drugs." Aaron kissed her again. "You threatened to rip my dick off if I didn't get you drugs."

Sonny sniffled. *They're my favorite couple. Time for a blessing.* He thought for a moment, trying to find the right words. He had already put protective spells all over Wendy's nursery and Gemma's nest, but those were short term.

He leaned down and kissed Wendy's soft forehead. "May you discover yourself early in life." He kissed her again. "May you have a kind heart." He kissed her one more time. "May you find joy always."

He felt his intentions settle into her, and her eyes fluttered open. She watched him for a moment, mouth pursed, then closed her eyes again, settling into sleep.

Sonny looked up. Gemma and Aaron were watching him with tears in their eyes.

"You blessed her?" Aaron pulled him into a hug. "Thank you, Sonny."

"Of course, I blessed her. What kind of godparent would I be if I didn't?" Sonny huffed. "Now, I need to go hunt up my honey bear. The air is swirling with energy and intention. I want my damn proposal."

Gemma blew him a kiss. "You're so romantic. Text us when it happens. We love you."

Sonny hugged them both and reluctantly handed Wendy over to them.

He left the room and wandered down the hall, stopping in surprise when he saw Leo and Myrtle both half asleep in the waiting room.

Sonny shook his head. "You two stayed behind? It's been hours."

"How are you so full of energy?" Leo rubbed sleep from his eyes.

"It's Ostara." Myrtle stood up, stretching her back. "It's urging us to move forward, plant our roots, and plan our futures." She winked at Sonny. "I think Sonny's a little more excited about this year's Ostara than usual."

Sonny hugged her. "I love you so much, Myrtle. You're my real mom, okay?"

She squeezed him tightly. "You can bet your boysenberries I am. I already reported Cynthia's actions to the Witches Council. They were furious, but enough of that. How's the baby?"

"Sleepy and well-fed." Sonny bounced on his feet. "Wendy is adorable, and I already blessed her. It's an Ostara blessing too, so it's even stronger."

Myrtle's eyes brightened. She loved giving blessings. Well, she also loved making digestive potions. They were her two favorite spells. "I'll need to give a blessing too."

Better than a digestive potion, Sonny thought.

She patted his cheek and started walking away. "That little girl will have a lot of witches standing in line to offer their own blessings, so I need to make mine the best."

Sonny rolled his eyes, then turned to Leo. He grinned and wiggled his brows. "I want my proposal, honey bear. Right now."

Leo chuckled. "I have it all planned out, sunshine.

We need incense and candles. Myrtle is going to do an Ostara scrying for us. Then, we're going on a short trip to Grandpa and Grandma's farm. I want to show you my favorite spots out in the woods around the farmhouse so we can appreciate and honor the spring. That's where I'm going to propose. I can be patient. I promise."

Sonny shook his head. "I can't. All you shifters have influenced me too much. I want my proposal now. The rest can come after."

Leo groaned. "Coleen will murder me if I fuck this up. You have no idea the amount of planning that has gone into this."

Sonny sat on his bear's lap and kissed him. "I'll protect you."

Leo gave him a soft look and buried his hand in the pocket of his jeans. A few seconds later, he pulled out a silver ring covered in delicately carved peppermint leaves.

Sonny's eyes watered. *Peppermint to summon happiness and positivity.* It was absolutely perfect for him.

Leo held the ring up. "I've been carrying this around for a month. I know peppermint is your favorite herb, and it brings happiness, just like you."

Sonny blinked away his tears. "It's beautiful."

Leo cupped his chin and tilted his face up. "Sonny, will you spend this year with me, learning what love and mating truly are?"

Sonny smiled widely. This moment and Leo's words felt right. "Yes."

Leo swallowed hard. "Then next year, at Beltane, will you honor me with a handfasting and permanently bind your soul to mine?"

Sonny smiled and held his finger up for Leo to slide the ring on. "There's nothing I'd enjoy more."

A few hours later, they sat on the sofa in their home. Sonny should have been sleeping away exhaustion, but he had never felt so energized.

Myrtle sat across the coffee table from them. The surface had been cleared away, and the items for the scrying were laid in front of them. Sonny had always thought it fitting that his own scrying skills resembled Myrtle's rather than his father's.

Myrtle's scrying bowl was made of black obsidian and well used. She had placed quartz crystals all around her bowl and the smudge stick to the right.

She picked the smudge stick up. "I made this especially for your Ostara scrying. It's made of mint for cleansing, lemongrass for passion and fidelity, and mugwort to induce the scrying." She closed her eyes. "I'll focus my intention now."

Sonny felt the pull of her magic moving from her soul into the smudge stick.

A moment later, she lit the end and waved it around her head. She passed it to him, and he waved it around his own head, then Leo's, before passing it back to her.

A thrumming filled the air as the intentional energy surrounded them.

Myrtle spoke in a low whisper, then snuffed the flame out in a small bowl of sand.

She snapped her fingers, and the white and brown

candles lined along the side of the table lit up. After that, time seemed to stand still.

Sonny didn't know if Leo felt the energy in the air, but for him, it was like a warm blanket on a cold day.

Moments or hours later, Myrtle's eyes popped open, and they all stared into the scrying bowl. The water showed an image of Leo and Sonny sitting together on a swing. They smiled and laughed together as they spoke, and it took a moment for Sonny to notice Leo's hand resting on his rounded belly in the image.

Myrtle grinned. "I declare you two thick-headed lovebirds are mates."

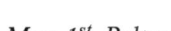

May 1st, Beltane

SONNY SMOOTHED A HAND DOWN ONE OF HIS LIGHT green suspenders. He had surprised everyone by insisting on tan trousers and colorful suspenders for his formal engagement ceremony. Leo's grandpa had gifted him an adorable brown felt trilby hat that went perfectly with his engagement outfit.

He had made sure to have multiple outfits ready because he really never knew for sure how he would want to express himself until the last minute. *I look perfect.*

He spun around and watched his image in the mirror.

"Sunshine, you're beautiful." Leo's image moved to stand behind him in the mirror. He wore a white dress shirt, a bright green vest, and light brown dress pants.

"Yummy bear." Sonny licked his lips. "You look delicious."

Leo's eyes sparkled with mischief. "We can be late, right?"

"No." Coleen pushed into the bedroom. "You two don't have time for a quickie right now. We're on a schedule." Leo's sister looked beautiful in her light blue dress.

Sonny shoved Leo aside and held his arms out. "Hug time, Coleen."

She laughed and hugged him. "You look lovely, Sonny."

He thought of everything she had done for him and Leo and hugged her tightly. "Thank you. For everything. I love Leo, and we would have figured things out, but all of this is my dream. It's always been my dream."

She kissed the top of his head. "It's what family is for. You're my little brother now."

He swallowed back tears and let her go. "Okay. Let's do this."

Coleen smiled at him, then shoved Leo. "Why can't you be nice like Sonny?"

Leo rolled his eyes. "Fuck off."

She ignored him. "Alright. Myrtle is already waiting, and the family is gathered. I know this is typically just for the immediate family, but the Rocchi clan doesn't fully understand that concept."

Sonny giggled. "Everyone's here, aren't they?"

"Yep." She shrugged. "They'll be here again next year."

She grabbed both of their hands and tugged them from the room.

"Is the picnic ready?" Sonny asked, shooting a wink at Leo. *I can't wait to get my honey bear alone.*

"Yes," Coleen said, waving toward the picnic tables near the park. "Tilisha and some of the others have everything ready."

Sonny smiled when he saw that the May Day festivities were already in full swing. Young men and women were already dancing around a large decorated maypole, and Sonny could hear music and laughter from where they stood.

"This way, Sonny." Coleen tugged on him again.

They walked deeper into the park until they came across a small clearing. It was full of bear shifters. Most were dressed as nicely as Coleen, but a few were in their bear forms.

Miles sat atop a brown bear's back and had Ravenpaw and Flufflepuff perched in front of him. He waved and grinned. "Looking good, Sonny!"

Leo sniffed. "I see how I rank."

Aaron whistled. "Leo is so hot."

Sonny snickered. "There, do you feel better?"

Leo gave him a prim look. "Yes."

Myrtle waved at them. "Come along, you two."

Coleen escorted them to the front of the crowd and

then left them to stand in front of Myrtle.

Myrtle wore her best dress and her long hair was decorated with pink and blue flowers. She gave Sonny a fond look, then winked at Leo.

Sonny grabbed Leo's hand and squeezed it. His mate was shaking.

"My Sonny and his catbear." Myrtle held up three loose ribbons. "A green ribbon, so that you may share of yourself freely, so that your happiness knows no bounds, and so that your union may be nourishing to you both. A light blue ribbon, so that you may always learn from one another, so that you may depend on one another, and so that you may be open about your desires. A white ribbon to symbolize your new beginnings and a hope that your union may be full of spirit."

Sonny almost gasped at the thrum of power he felt radiating from Myrtle. He had been to several engagement bindings in the past but had never felt this before.

She held the ribbons up. "I braid into these ribbons my hopes and wishes that you will help one another grow in spirit and wisdom, that you will support one another through daily actions and encouraging words, and that you will forge an unbreakable mating built of love and respect."

Myrtle's energy and love flowed through him and his eyes watered.

She placed the braided ribbons around their joined hands, tying them in a loose knot. "Today I bind you together, heart and mind, for a year and a day."

CHAPTER 23

MAY 1ST, BELTANE - ONE YEAR LATE

*L*eo warmed his hands near the bonfire Thorwald and Aaron had built in the largest clearing of the park. The past year had been the best of his life. He had thought he'd resent having to wait to make things completely official with Sonny, but the time they had taken had allowed the love he felt to deepen.

He *knew* Sonny in a way no one else did. He knew his strong, pure spirit and utterly beautiful heart. He knew the way his body felt and tasted and what made Sonny wail in pleasure. He knew what Sonny wanted in life, what he valued, and what he believed in. He knew his mate.

Now it's time to honor him. Leo rubbed his bare belly. He had gotten a little plumper over the last year. Sonny's cooking was too good to not indulge; however, he didn't feel even a little self-conscious standing there with only a pair of loose brown pants on and his chest, gut, and feet bare. Loving Sonny had helped him love himself too.

Also, almost everyone was equally bare. *It's a good thing that shifters are familiar with nudity or my family would be teasing the hell out of me right now.*

Leo's whole family - cousins, aunts, and uncles included – mingled around the fire with Leo and Sonny's friends. A small platform sat near the trees, and a band played lively music.

Several couples were dancing, including his parents and Rosemarie and Kate. They twirled around the fire, laughing and singing along.

A few of the humans and vampires in the crowd looked a little uncomfortable, but they were making an effort not to stare at the bare chests and naked breasts surrounding them.

Niels stood beside him, clapping along to the music. "This is great. I never would have thought witches and shifters would get along so well. Is that Philip, your best friend from high school?"

Leo grinned and waved at the lion shifter standing near the stage. "Yeah, he flew out to be here."

Coleen ran past them, wringing her hands. "Damn it, Uncle Lyle already shifted and got into the beer."

Leo looked around. Several of his family and friends were in bear form, romping around and enjoying the wild energy pulsing through the earth beneath them.

Burkhart lumbered by in his bear form, Flufflepuff and Ravenpaw riding on his back. Ravenpaw had outgrown Fluff over the last year. The two cats made a striking pair.

"A wild party is an odd way to start a wedding, isn't it?" Niels asked.

Leo winced, privately agreeing. The actual handfasting would happen tomorrow, a year and a day from when they bound themselves together.

A flash of deep green caught his eye, and Leo sighed happily. "This is the *perfect* way to start a wedding."

Sonny danced with Aaron and Gemma, and his heated gaze was focused right on Leo. He looked delicious in his long emerald tulle skirt and bare chest. A crown of ivy sat atop his brown hair, and his bare feet made Leo's dick hard. *Damn, bare feet shouldn't be that arousing, should they?*

Sonny crooked a finger and licked his lips.

"Gotta go." Leo left Niels laughing and ran for his mate.

He didn't get far. Thorwald grabbed his shoulder, pulling him to the stop. "Where you heading so fast?"

His dancing eyes told Leo his brother knew exactly where Leo was going. "Don't make me eat your face, Thor."

Thorwald threw his head back, laughing. "Fine. Go on, little brother."

Leo pushed past him and finally reached his mate.

Sonny draped his arms over Leo's shoulders, and Leo lifted him up against his body. He could feel Sonny's hardness beneath the bunched-up tulle.

"Why haven't you worn that skirt before, sunshine?"

Leo nipped Sonny's neck, then licked over his mating mark. "You should wear it every day."

"Then it wouldn't be special." Sonny arched his neck. "It's Beltane night."

Leo hummed. "The goddess marries her love, and the earth gives birth."

Sonny pressed his lips to Leo, then bit his bottom lip. "I need you."

Leo held back a smile. Witches really did have a heat like shifters. The past few months had been a lot of fun. "Here? We're supposed to be celebrating."

"Yes," Sonny practically hissed. "Can't you feel all this energy? I need you inside me."

Leo held him close and looked around the park. "It's really crowded."

Sonny nipped his ear. "Leo. Now."

"Fuck." Leo carried Sonny as far away from the crowd as he could, but he knew there were plenty of shifters roaming the woods. *Who the hell cares? My witch needs me.*

He set Sonny down next to a large oak with a hollowed trunk. The tree wouldn't be enough cover, but there were a few bushes that would hide them. Leo had to admit the thought that they could be heard or seen was a tiny bit thrilling.

Sonny hooked an arm around his neck. "It feels different this year."

Leo swallowed hard when Sonny gently bit his neck. "Yeah. Last year was good, but this... This is different. It's stronger somehow."

"Uh-huh." Sonny tugged Leo down with him until they both lay on the hard, slightly wet ground.

Sonny didn't seem a bit concerned about lying in the dirt and leaves, and Leo had to admit his mate looked lovely spread out in the shadows. The lighted path was far away now, but Leo saw well enough in the dark.

Sonny watched him with heated eyes as he raised his tulle skirt above his waist. He was bare beneath. He hooked a leg over one of his arms and completely bared his hole.

"Sunshine." Leo heard the raw need in his own voice.

Sonny stroked his dick, then ran one hand to his hole. "Notice something different?"

Leo knelt between his legs. "Your favorite plug. You're ready, aren't you?"

Sonny tapped the end of the plug and whimpered, legs trembling. "Please, Leo."

"Get yourself ready for me, sunshine." Leo pushed his pants down and started stroking his dick as he watched his witch writhe on the ground.

Sonny pulled the plug out, then pushed it back in. "It feels so good."

"I'll feel better."

Sonny slowly removed the plug, then quickly pushed a finger into his tight hole. He groaned and added a second finger.

His hips bucked as he began to fuck his fingers, and he moaned at the steadily building pleasure.

Leo licked his lips and stroked his dick faster. "Sonny."

Sonny panted hard but removed his fingers from his lubed, stretched ass. "I want a warm, hard cock inside me, not my fingers."

Leo growled and easily picked him up, drawing him closer. He braced his back against the tree and arranged Sonny to straddle his lap.

He cupped Sonny's ass and arched his hips, rubbing his dick over Sonny's wet hole. Leo cupped Sonny's chin and tilted his face up. "You're my heart and my soul, Sonny. I love you beyond measure." His voice was uneven and gruff with excitement, even to his own ears.

Leo's mouth pressed against Sonny's, and he lost all ability to think. His hand on the back of Sonny's neck held him still so he could plunder the soft depths of his mate's mouth. His tongue wrapped around Sonny's, and he relished his witch's broken sigh.

Leo reached for Sonny's dick and stroked him once, using his thumb to rub at the pre-cum leaking from the head.

Sonny's groan was long and loud. He positioned himself over Leo's dick. "You're everything to me, Leo. You're my home."

Leo growled as Sonny started to lower himself onto Leo's dick. He gripped Sonny's hips and helped guide him until his ass settled on Leo's thighs.

Leo cupped the back of Sonny's neck again, and he kissed his mate as Sonny set a fast rhythm, riding him hard.

It wasn't long before Sonny came, groaning deeply as he shuddered above Leo, his dick shooting into the tulle of his skirt.

Leo grasped Sonny's hips and moved faster, pounding into him. He pressed his mouth against his neck, and as Leo came deep inside him, he buried his fangs into Sonny's neck, renewing their claiming mark.

Sonny screamed, body trembling as he came again, the muscles of his ass clenching around Leo.

As he came down from his high, Leo tightened his arms around Sonny and kissed the top of his head. He smelled of honey, sunshine, and sex. *My favorite scent*

"Leo." Sonny panted, still working to catch his breath.

He pulled Leo into another kiss, and Leo went willingly, his mate's taste heating him from the inside out. No matter how many times they kissed, Sonny's taste would always bring Leo to his knees. *Forever and always.*

CHAPTER 24

"I can't believe you came back to the bonfire smelling like sex and covered in leaves and sticks," Coleen hissed as she worked at tying Leo's tie. Leo and his siblings were getting ready for the handfasting in Myrtle's apartment. Leo was wearing a classic gray suit and pale blue tie.

"I can dress myself," he mumbled, then quieted when she glared at him. "Sorry." Leo arched his sore back. Fucking against a tree may not have been the smartest thing in the world, but making Sonny happy was worth a little pain.

Ravenpaw looked up from his spot on Toddlebug's tree. Their cat wore a pale blue silk bowtie around his fluffy neck. Flufflepuff would be wearing a matching one.

"Give him a break." Burkhart settled his hands on their sister's tense shoulders. "Last night was kinda wild. Let's just say I never knew witches tasted so good."

"Who were you nibbling?" Niels asked, fiddling with his hair in the mirror.

"Sonny's cousin Giles." Burkhart grinned and wiggled his brows. "He's a lot of fun. We're getting together again tonight."

A surprising number of Sonny's relatives were coming to the handfasting. His parents were not, and Leo was pretty damn happy about that. He didn't know if he could control his mom if Cynthia Thornton showed up.

"You know Giles is going back to England tomorrow, right?" Coleen said, glaring at Burkhart over her shoulder. "Put your shirt on."

Burkhart frowned and looked around the living room. "I lost it."

"How can you lose a shirt?" Coleen left Leo alone and went to help Burkhart dig through Myrtle's clutter.

Leo looked around "Where are Thor and Rosie?"

"Oh, damn. Did we lose them too?" Burkhart winced and spun around the room. "Marco?"

"Polo," Thorwald sang out as he came in the front door, Rosemarie at his back.

"Oh, thank the gods." Burkhart held up his shirt. "They're not lost, and here's my shirt. How does Myrtle find anything in here?"

Leo shrugged. "She has a system."

"Are you all ready yet?" Katrin asked from the door. "Everyone's here and the chanting has started." Leo's mom looked beautiful in her yellow dress.

"We're almost ready." Coleen clapped her hands. "Everyone is dressed. Where are the flowers?"

"Here." Rosemarie held up an armful of boxes. "There are boutonnieres for all of us and a flower crown for Leo."

Leo looked up. "Huh?"

Rosemarie handed him a loose crown of myrtle branches and woodruff flowers. "Sonny made it for you."

Leo plopped it on his head. "Okay."

Coleen sighed and reached up to straighten it. "Really, Leo."

"Sonny made each of our boutonnieres." Rosemarie smiled. "He labeled them and everything. Here, Coleen."

Coleen took her boutonniere and laughed. "Honeysuckle? Sonny is such an asshole."

"Huh?" Thorwald asked, head tilted.

Coleen rolled her eyes. "Honeysuckle is supposed to summon wet dreams. Sonny and I were talking at lunch the other day... Oh, never mind."

Leo grinned. "Remember when you didn't think he liked you?"

She smiled softly. "Yeah."

Katrin sighed. "Again. Everyone's waiting on you all."

"We're going." Niels finished pinning on his boutonniere of hawthorn flowers and tugged Thorwald with him out the door.

Coleen straightened his flower crown one more

time, then kissed his cheek. "I'll take Ravenpaw with me." She picked the cat up and left.

Burkhart grinned, waiting until she was gone to tilt Leo's crown to the side before running out the door with Rosemarie.

Katrin shook her head. "Come on, son. I'll fix your flowers."

Leo snorted. "I never thought you'd have to say that to me."

"You're the one who was fortunate enough to mate a witch."

"Not just any witch." Leo smiled softly. "My sunshine."

He left with his mom, and they held hands as they walked into the park.

The silence between them was a happy one. He'd spent a lot more time with his parents this past year. It had been important to Sonny.

They reached the very center of the park to find a huge circle of people. A loud, steady chanting filled the air. Leo didn't know the words spoken, but even he could feel the power behind them.

He shook his head. "Damn, there are a lot more people here than I thought there'd be."

Katrin nodded. "All our family is here, but more Blackwoods and Whitmores showed up. I think Myrtle put the fear of the goddess in them." She eyed him. "Are you nervous?"

Leo shook his head. "Nope. This ceremony is the next step in celebrating our mating. I already know Sonny is mine and I'm his."

Katrin squeezed his head. "I'll go stand with your father. We love you, Leo."

"Love you too, Mom."

He slowly made his way through the circle of people, happily accepting the hugs and pats on the back. Normally, the circle would be clearly formed with a side for each groom, but they hadn't realized Sonny's extended family would show up. *Meh, Grandma and Grandpa would have wanted to be on Sonny's side anyway.*

By the time he pushed to the center of the circle, Sonny was there, Flufflepuff and Ravenpaw at his feet.

Leo took his time looking his mate over. Sonny wore a surprisingly simple antique white dress with a crocheted top and a tattered skirt. He carried a bouquet of Blackwood roses, *their* Blackwood roses. A flower crown of myrtle branches and primroses sat on his head. *Beautiful.*

Myrtle stood beside him, wearing her best robes. She grinned. "About time. Let's get moving, you two. I want some cake."

Sonny rolled his eyes and reached for Leo with his free hand. "You better listen to her, honey bear. I can hear her stomach growling from here."

Leo took his hands and brought them to his lips. Sonny smiled and pressed a kiss to Leo's knuckles in return.

Myrtle held her hands up. "As most of you know, handfasting is a witch ceremony that symbolizes the love between a couple and forever binds together the souls of true mates. It is not to be taken lightly. Leo and

Sonny have spent the past year learning about one another and have chosen to take the next step. I am honored to share this with my Sonny and his catbear."

She took their joined hands in her own. Leo shivered as a shot of something whipped through him. Myrtle's eyes seemed to glow brighter, and a soft white light surrounded her hands.

"I bless these hands. These are the hands of your truest companion. The hands of the person you will grow old with. The hands that will work with you to build your future. I bless you by the earth, air, water, and fire that form the goddess. I bless you with wisdom, passion, love, and kindness."

Leo gasped as power flowed from her hands and into them. Myrtle's blessings seemed to settle into his bones.

She released their hands and waved for Miles to step forward. Sonny's apprentice was dressed in a suit of his own and handed Myrtle a cord of three thick strands braided together.

She wrapped the cord tightly around their wrists. "A blue cord so that you may be steadfast and true. A yellow cord so that your love may be a light in the darkness. A gray cord so that your union may weather every storm of life. I bind you together, body, heart, and soul."

The chanting grew louder, and the air around them almost seemed to shimmer.

Myrtle held her hands up and the chanting stopped. The sudden silence was deafening. "Bring your blessings forward."

Aaron and Gemma stepped forward. Little Wendy looked lovely in her frilled dress and perched on Gemma's hip. Tears filled Aaron's eyes. "I wish only happiness and joy for both of you, but we bless you with our constant friendship. We will *always* stand beside you no matter what you face."

Sonny's lip trembled, and Aaron and Gemma stepped back.

Leo's grandparents stepped forward. Janine smiled through her tears. "We wish wisdom and insight for you both, but we bless you with our experience of life. Ronald and I have had our trials, and we'll share the nuggets of wisdom we've learned through the years. We'll be here whenever you need us."

Leo swallowed his tears and squeezed Sonny's hands. They shared a smile.

His grandparents stepped back, and Leo's parents stepped forward. Katrin gave them a fierce smile. "We wish strength and passion for you both, and we bless you with our protection and unconditional love. You are both our children, and we'll fight to the death for each of you."

Sonny sniffled and they stepped back. Each of Leo's siblings came forward and offered their well wishes and blessings, each surprisingly heartfelt.

Then almost every single person present came forward, and at one point, they had to jump over a handmade broom. Leo still wasn't sure why, but Sonny cried when they did it. The blessings themselves took a while, and the number of fertility blessings was a little alarming. *Maybe diapers really are a good handfasting gift.*

Eventually, they worked through most of the guests, and Myrtle held her hands up again. "May the goddess hear our blessings and offer Leo and Sonny her own. The handfasting is done. Sonny and Leo are bound to one another, and you, their loved ones, are here to celebrate the joy the day brings." She grinned. "Let's go eat."

∿

AN HOUR LATER, LEO SAT ON A BLANKET IN THE GRASS, Sonny at his side. Flufflepuff and Ravenpaw both sprawled beside them, cuddled close together.

The reception, or feast as Myrtle kept calling it, was in another part of the park. Picnic tables and blankets were spread all around, and the same band from the night before played.

Sonny held Wendy balanced on her feet. "You can do it, Wendy. I'll get you walking, then nothing can stop us from taking over the apartment complex. Everyone shall bow to your cuteness."

Leo snorted. "They already do."

Sonny grinned. "You're right." He gave Leo a serious look. "We got a lot of fertility blessings today."

Leo blinked innocently. "Yes, I suppose we did."

"The gift table is full of baby supplies, mostly from your family."

"Imagine that."

Sonny gave him an exasperated look. "Are you saying you want to start trying for a baby?"

Leo rubbed his chin. "Are *you* saying you want to try for a baby?"

"Oh, for the love of –"

The music suddenly cut off, drawing their eyes.

"If I can have your attention." Thorwald waved his hands from the band's platform. "We have a special treat for our beloved Sonny. If you'll direct your attention to the center of the clearing, you'll see a certain rabbit shifter on a picnic table."

Sonny gasped and bounced in place. "Finally!"

"Is this the only reason you wanted a handfasting?" Leo asked suspiciously.

"I don't have the time to answer that." Sonny helped Wendy clap. "It's time for the bunny boogie."

Aaron was in his shifted form, but he wasn't alone. Gemma stood beside him on the picnic table and several shifted bears stood to each side. Leo recognized his parents, grandparents, and siblings.

Sonny's eyes widened when Thorwald shucked his clothes and shifted, joining the group. "What's going on here?"

"Well," Leo slowly drawled. "They've had the whole year to practice."

"Practice?" Sonny squealed. "Are they all going to do it?"

The band started playing a fast, rolling tune and the dance began. Each of the shifters followed Aaron's movements, with first their paws in the air. They shook them to the right, and Sonny cackled, sounding suspiciously like Myrtle.

Then Aaron and the others shook their paws to the left. Sonny bounced again. "It's coming, it's coming."

Aaron's furry little body shimmied, ears and tail bouncing. The others followed suit, the bears a lot clumsier than Aaron and Gemma. Then they shook their rear ends wildly, back and forth.

Aaron's little cotton tail twerked in the air, and Sonny lost it. He laughed so hard he cried. Leo couldn't help but laugh with him. If one dance made his mate so happy, he'd make Aaron and the others dance it every day.

Wendy giggled and clapped.

"See Mommy and Daddy, Wendy? There are all your bear friends too. Aren't they perfect?" Sonny asked. "Aren't they the best? One day, you'll dance with them too, right? For Uncle Sonny?"

Leo leaned back, smiling widely. *Damn, life is good.*

PART IV
CARROT CAKE AND A WITCH'S SURPRISE

Holiday Omegas: Book Four

CHAPTER 25

JUNE

*S*onny cursed as he hugged the toilet and threw up for the second time that morning. His head pounded and all he wanted to do was curl up in his husband's lap and sleep. *Stupid stomach needs to calm the hell down.*

A bout of dizziness hit him, making him moan. *I'm sorry, stupid stomach. You're the boss, I swear.*

A soft, warm weight settled against his back, and the dizziness started to fade. His familiar, Flufflepuff, rubbed her head against his side, her purring sending small, soothing vibrations through him.

Sonny almost moaned when a cool cloth was pressed to his head.

He glanced to his left. "Did I wake you?"

Leo rolled his eyes. "Seriously? You're clearly feeling like shit and you're afraid you woke me up?"

"Don't yell at me," Sonny said, lip trembling. He knew Leo wasn't mad at him, but damn if he could control his emotions right then.

Leo's eyes softened, and he rubbed Sonny's back. "I'm sorry, sunshine. Is your stomach feeling better? Let me help you."

Sonny let Leo pull him up and hold him steady as he brushed his teach and washed his face. "Carry me to the bed?"

"My pleasure." Leo scooped him up and carried him back into their room. Ravenpaw, Sonny's large, fluffy black cat watched them from the four-poster bed.

Leo settled Sonny in his spot, and Sonny curled around his pillow, sleep pulling at him. Flufflepuff hopped up and curled against his back again, steadily purring and offering her strength.

He vaguely heard Leo moving around the room, but Sonny felt it when Leo lit the first of the pre-spelled blue candles. A jolt of healing calm settled in his stomach, and he started to drift off to sleep.

Sonny rubbed his face against his pillow. "Don't light the green ones anymore." *No need for fertility candles*, he thought wryly.

He fell asleep to Leo's rumbling laughter.

By the time he woke up again, morning sunshine poured through the wide windows. Sonny and Leo's bedroom was cluttered with books, candles, and other knick-knacks. Colorful strands of glass hung from the ceiling and caught the sunbeams, sending shards of colored light to dance across the walls.

Home, he thought, sighing at the peace that filled him.

The closet doors stood open, and Sonny winced at

the sight of all his clothes and shoes. *I may have a problem.* The light glinted off the shiny gold-heeled sandals he'd bought the day before. *What am I saying? Shoes are life. There's no problem here.*

A warm breeze rustled his hair, and he noticed the balcony doors stood open. Sonny turned onto his back and pulled Fluff into his arms to pet as he watched the light dance across Leo's broad, tan shoulders.

His mate stood on the balcony with his morning coffee. Ravenpaw wound between Leo's bare feet, tail high in the air. Sonny loved that Leo didn't even seem to notice his nakedness most of the time. His mate used to be so self-conscious of his soft stomach, but now, he barely remembered to wear shorts on the balcony.

Leo's damn shoulders were too appealing. Sonny checked the time, then snapped his fingers, lighting the three red candles spread around the room.

He set Flufflepuff on Leo's pillow and slid out of bed, happy that his stomach was settled. For some reason, it always chose three in the morning to be a dickhead.

Sonny snuck behind Leo and wrapped his arms around his mate's waist, hugging him tightly and breathing in his warm, masculine scent. "Good morning."

Leo set his coffee on the rail and turned around, pulling Sonny close and kissing him. Sonny enjoyed the press of his mate's large body against his own.

"You lit the red candles, didn't you?" Leo asked, amusement filling his voice. "Do we have time?"

Sonny leaned back, glaring. "There's always time for morning sex."

Leo's laughter shook them both. "What was I thinking?"

"It's okay," Sonny said, patting Leo's cheek. "No one can be *completely* perfect."

Leo leaned down and nibbled on Sonny's neck. "You're the tastiest treat, sunshine. What would I do without you?"

Sonny gently bit Leo's chin. "Die alone, because I will haunt your ass if you try to mate someone else if I die. Now, we have a little over an hour before we both need to leave. Get your ass in gear. I want morning fun times and strawberry pancakes."

Leo hummed low in his throat and pulled them into the room as Sonny pressed kisses to his shoulders. "I live to serve my mate."

"Good answer." Sonny trailed his mouth down Leo's chest. "Why do you always taste so good? You do it on purpose, don't you?"

Leo's laugh ended on a gasp when Sonny teased his nipples. He groaned and shivered when Sonny's teeth tugged gently on one nub.

"Sonny," he said, voice rough.

Sonny ignored him and slid to his knees. He pulled Leo's sleep shorts down to free his dick. "Yummiest honey bear in the whole world. Love you."

Leo ran his hand through Sonny's hair. "I love you too, sunshine."

Sonny wrapped his hands around Leo's dick and tugged, pumping him hard. When his mate's groans hit a certain familiar pitch, Sonny leaned forward and sucked the tip into his mouth as he continued to stroke Leo. *Yep, tastiest man in the world.*

"Need you," Leo said, head falling back when Sonny swallowed him deep.

Sonny snorted a laugh when Leo pulled him to his feet. "Impatient much?"

Leo hummed in agreement and kissed him, licking the precum off his lips. His hands slid down Sonny's back and cupped his ass, pulling their hips together before picking him up and setting him on the dresser.

Leo slid Sonny's silky pajama bottoms off and leaned down to suck the tip of Sonny's dick. "I'm not the only one with an addictive taste, sunshine."

Sonny wiggled his hips. "Inside me, please."

Leo smiled softly, then grabbed the lube. He pressed a finger against Sonny's pucker, slipping the tip in and making Sonny shiver with need.

Sonny panted and spread his legs wider as Leo pushed his finger deeper and trailed kisses along Sonny's neck, lingering over the mating mark on Sonny's neck.

Leo slid more fingers in, stretching Sonny, before angling his hips and slowly sinking into him.

They moved together slowly at first, but they fit too well and it felt too good to last long.

Leo moved faster and faster until Sonny's climax splattered them both with cum. Sonny's ass clenched around Leo's dick. Leo's growl made Sonny's dick harden again.

Leo let himself go, pounding in and out of Sonny's ass, shaking the dresser under them.

Sonny came again, and Leo followed, filling Sonny's ass.

They panted against each other for a few moments. "Pancakes, right?" Sonny asked, rubbing his face against Leo's shoulder.

Leo chuckled. "I love how you stick to a plan."

Sonny grinned and kissed Leo's own mating mark. "You shower and I'll cook."

"Yes, darling," Leo said with a smirk and slowly eased from his body. "Do you need anything first?"

"Nope." Sonny smacked Leo's bare ass as he walked past, making his mate yelp in surprise. "I got what I needed."

Leo laughed all the way to the bathroom.

Sonny slid on his robe and debated shutting the balcony doors before deciding to leave them open. The room smelled of sex now and could use some airing out.

The cats followed him downstairs, doing their best to murder him on the stairs as they darted between his feet.

He filled their feed bowls and refreshed their water before turning his attention to his own breakfast. He quickly brewed another pot of coffee for Leo and made himself a cup of red raspberry leaf tea, pre-spelled to treat nausea and mood swings.

Sonny sipped his tea, then put together the batter for the pancakes, adding his intentions for the day. "A little orange peel for centering and blessings and all the strawberries in the world because I need them." He popped a strawberry in his mouth and moaned, wiggling in happiness. "Also good for health, luck, and reinforcing love and romance."

And fertility, he added to himself, smiling at his secret. They had been eating strawberry pancakes every morning for two months now, only partially because Sonny had been craving them.

He walked onto the first story balcony and picked a few leaves of peppermint from his potted herb rack. "Can't forget the most important herb. Peppermint for love, healing, and energy."

Sonny had the table set and their breakfast laid out by the time Leo came down the stairs. His mate looked as yummy as ever in his work coveralls with the Rocci's Garage logo covering the back.

Leo gave him a kiss and held his chair for him as he sat. "This looks as good as always, love."

"I made a spinach basil lasagna for you to take in today." Sonny stuffed a strawberry in his mouth. Basil could be spelled to help with businesses and money making, so he usually tried to make dishes with it to send with Leo to his family's garage.

Fortunately, the family of bear shifters loved his cooking and were happy to have homemade lunches every Tuesday and Friday.

"That's Coleen's favorite." Leo methodically worked his way through his pancakes. "Thank you for taking care of us, sunshine."

Warmth filled Sonny at Leo's words. Sonny loved having a family to take care of. His mentor, Myrtle, would only let him coddle her so much before she yelled and threatened to turn him into a hamster.

"You're still planning on only working a half-day today, right?" Leo asked, eyes full of concern. "You've been working non-stop at the shop all summer, so you deserve the vacation."

Sonny nodded, trying to hide his excitement. Summer Solstice, known as Litha in witch society, was Sunday, and he and Leo were taking the weekend to visit Leo's grandparents on their farm. Sonny planned to tell Leo his secret on Sunday.

He had a special scrying and blessing to do on Litha this year.

"I'm all set for our long weekend. Tilisha and Devin are watching the shop tomorrow, and we're closed for Litha on Sunday and Monday. Everything's handled."

Sonny smiled when Leo scooped some of his strawberries onto Sonny's empty plate. He quickly ate them, relishing the sweet juiciness.

"Are you still happy with Devin?" Leo asked, smiling as he watched Sonny eat the last strawberry.

Sonny nodded and swallowed his bite. "He's good with customers and doesn't mind making most of the potions since Myrtle is retiring. That leaves Tilisha to handle the front register with Dev and me to spot her when we can."

At the beginning of the month, Sonny's mentor had finally made the decision to retire from the shop. They had already hired Devin and it had seemed like the right time. Myrtle had handed the reins over to Sonny and went on a long vacation to visit her sister on the coast.

Sonny missed her more than he wanted to admit, but she was coming back after Litha.

As soon as they finished breakfast, Leo stood and started gathering dishes. "I'll clean up and you go shower, sunshine. Do you mind if I take Ravenpaw with me to work today? You might need Flufflepuff if your stomach starts bothering you again."

Sonny watched the two cats lounging on the cat tree in front of the largest window in the living room. Fluff looked up and gave him a sweet look. She usually went with Leo so she could watch over him for Sonny.

"That will work," he said, finally. "Ravenpaw needs some Rocci family loving anyway."

He quickly showered and considered his clothes. It was going to be a warm summer day, and he was feeling particularly wonderful at the moment. "Today is a sundress kind of day."

He pulled out the long, blue, front button maxi dress with the large yellow flowers on it. *Definitely goes with the raffia heels and my gold hoop earrings*, he thought. *Time for a good day.*

BY NOON, SONNY WAS DROOPING. HE SAT IN ONE OF THE comfortable reading chairs in front of the window, Flufflepuff purring in his lap.

The shop had expanded over the last year. Instead of a cozy room with a few shelves of potions and tonics and a small display of baked goods, it was now a large open space with several racks of potions, tonics, and other pre-spelled items along with a small café style seating area. A few months ago, they had started serving fresh tea and now customers tended to linger a bit longer.

Devin gave him a concerned look and handed him a cup of his red raspberry leaf tea. "Are you sure you're okay?"

Sonny rolled his eyes. "I'll be okay. I just need to rest for a moment."

Tilisha leaned over the back of the chair. "That first trimester is a pain in the ass, isn't it?"

Sonny gave her his best innocent look. "I don't know what you're talking about."

She arched a brow. "Just make sure you rest when you're tired. Don't push yourself. Devin here is a half-way decent kitchen witch and can handle some of the baking by himself."

Devin gave her a dry look. "Gee, thanks, T."

The omega kitchen witch was a stark contrast to Tilisha's soft curves and warm brown skin. His tall, pale frame was all angles and edges. Their personalities, however, were very similar. The two were both smart, hardworking, and sarcastic as hell.

"Seriously, though, the store probably needs a break from all the fertility enhancing cakes and cookies you've been making anyway." Tilisha grinned. "Mrs. Daly isn't happy with you, by the way. She ate some of her daughter's carrot cake, and now they're both pregnant and due at the same time."

Sonny held his hands up. "That's not my fault. Missy and her mate have been trying to have a baby for a long time. I just helped. It's not my fault Missy didn't tell her not to eat the cake."

Tilisha shook her head and went to help a customer.

Devin gave him another concerned look. "Really, though, I can handle more of the baking if you need me to."

"Thank you, Dev." Sonny polished off his cup of tea and reluctantly stood. "Now, Fluff and I have an appointment with my apprentice."

Devin took his mug and handed him a bag. "I made you some oatmeal cookies last night. Have a good weekend, boss, and don't worry about the shop."

Sonny gave him a suspicious look. "What kind of oatmeal cookies?"

"Cookies to aid in strength and, uh…" He looked at Sonny's abdomen. "Other things."

Sonny pulled the omega into a hug and squeezed him tightly. "Thank you, Devin."

The other witch flushed. "No problem. Enjoy Litha, Sonny."

"You too." Sonny frowned as he picked up Flufflepuff. Normally, he celebrated the summer solstice with Myrtle, his best friend Aaron, and now that he had mated, Leo. It felt odd not having everyone there.

Myrtle was at the coast, and Aaron, his mate, and their daughter had left town yesterday. His friend hadn't explained where he was going. In fact, Aaron had been acting shifty for a few weeks now.

Sonny shook his thoughts away and waved to Tilisha before leaving the shop. The walk to the apartment complex wasn't long, but it didn't help Sonny's fatigue.

Miles was already in the apartment. Sonny's young apprentice was playing with his familiar, Cookie, in the living room.

He looked up, smile fading. "You don't look so good."

Sonny slipped his heels off and sat on the couch. "I'm just a little tired. Give me a minute and we'll begin your lesson. We're covering pre-spelling items today."

Miles frowned. "I think we should have a break today."

He pulled Sonny from the couch and led him to the kitchen. "Sit at the bar, and I'll make your favorite treat."

Sonny smiled and did as he was told. "What's that?"

"Lately, you've been eating a lot of carrot cake." Miles tapped his chin. "Sugar to attract what you want. In this case, I want you to feel better. Then oat flour for comfort, and carrots for... fertility." He gave Sonny a suspicious look. "You're pregnant, aren't you?"

Sonny snickered. "I've been eating spelled carrot cake and spelled strawberries, lighting spelled green candles, and completing a morning fertility blessing every day for two months. I'm pregnant."

Miles grinned and hugged him. "You and Leo will be good dads. Now, I'm adding chamomile for health and protection. That will go okay in a carrot cake, right?"

Sonny shrugged. "I don't know. I've never added it before. Only one way to find out."

Miles nodded and started gathering ingredients. "One special carrot cake coming up."

CHAPTER 26

*L*eo whistled as he carried Ravenpaw into Rocci's Garage. The coolness of the air conditioner made him sigh with pleasure. His coveralls were not meant for hot summer days.

Coleen looked up from her laptop and smiled before holding out her arms. "Hand over Ravenpaw. I need some company up front today."

Leo scowled and set Ravenpaw on the front desk. "Maybe he wants to spend the day with me."

Ravenpaw's tail swished as he walked to Coleen. The blue and gold, Ravenclaw-themed bowtie looked particularly good against his thick black fur. He climbed into Coleen's arms and turned to stare at Leo.

"Well," Leo huffed, trying to hide his smile. "See who you like at lunch time. I'm the one with the cat treats."

Coleen gave him a smug look. "I have some in my desk."

Leo turned on his heel and stalked into the next

room. His dad was just leaving the breakroom and almost bumped into him.

Jesse steadied Leo as he nearly tipped over. "Sorry about that, Leo." He gave him an eager look. "Has Sonny finally told –"

"No," Leo interrupted, sulking. "He still hasn't said anything and Litha is on Sunday. Myrtle said that the scrying should be done on Litha for the best results, and Sonny hasn't even mentioned it."

Jesse rubbed his arm. "Sonny probably has a plan. We'll just surprise him before he surprises you."

Leo rubbed his nose. Shifters had a keen sense of smell, and Leo had noticed Sonny's delicious scent had changed a couple weeks ago. His mate was pregnant. "Can I ask you something?"

Jesse gave him an understanding look and pulled him into the breakroom. "What's wrong?"

"What if I'm not a good dad?" Leo swallowed hard. "I'm good with all the little Rocchi kids and Aaron and Gemma's daughter, but what if I fuck up? This is *my* child. I'm scared, Dad."

Jesse sat him in a chair at the break table, then sat beside him. "I'm going to be honest, Leo. You *are* going to fuck up."

Leo glared at his dad. "This is the worse pep talk ever."

Jesse chuckled. "Every parent fucks up at some point. Do you know how many times I dropped Burkhart? Frankly, I'm surprised he's as smart as he is. Then there's all the times we forgot to pick you and Thorwald up from daycare or school. After a while, you two started taking your afterschool snacks with you in the morning. Plus, do you remember when I told Coleen's first boyfriend how often she had to shave her legs? She didn't talk to me for a month."

"Oh fuck." Leo buried his face in his hands. "My child's going to hate me."

Jesse patted his back. "Do you hate me?"

Leo peeked through his fingers. "Not all the time."

"Why not?"

"Because I know you love me, even if you and Mom do stupid stuff sometimes."

Jesse smiled. "Exactly. As long as you love that kid unconditionally, the rest can be figured out."

Leo leaned back in his seat and stared at the ceiling. "I already love the baby unconditionally. It's part of me and Sonny, but it's more than that." He looked at his dad. "The baby's our family."

Jesse gave him a soft look. "That's as it should be. Now, your grandma called and told me everything's set up for the Litha celebration on Sunday."

"Do you think Sonny will mind us inviting everyone?"

Jesse shrugged. "He hasn't minded us being there before."

"That doesn't make me feel better."

"Here." Jesse picked up the lasagna carrier. "I'll take care of that for you. Go and relax for a minute. It's going to be busy today."

"Don't eat our lunch for breakfast," Leo warned as he headed to his station. His dad was right though. It was going to be a busy day.

Leo lit the pink, black, and white candles Sonny had given him a while ago. *Pink for harmony, white to dispel negativity, and black for protection.* He had no idea if they worked or not, but he had promised Sonny that he would light them every morning.

That done, he started reviewing his appointments for the day. The morning would bring two oil changes, one new fuel tank, and one set of tires.

A moment later, his brother Burkhart came in. "Hey, Leo. Has Sonny—"

"No." Leo threw a bottle of water at his eldest brother. "Why do you all ask that every morning?"

Burkhart easily caught the bottle and took a drink. "We all scent him, and we want to cuddle and pamper him. It's what we do with pregnant people in our family. You know that." He tilted his head. "Well, except for Aunt Tula. When she's pregnant, she'll cut your nuts off if you try to cuddle her."

Leo shuddered. During her last pregnancy, Leo had made the mistake of trying to bring her a plate of food. "Don't remind me."

Thorwald yawned as he stumbled into the garage. "Hey, has Sonny said any—"

Leo growled and shoved his sleepy brother into Burkhart. "Be a good brother, Burk, and throttle him, please?"

"With pleasure." Burkhart laughed and maneuvered Thorwald into a headlock so he could mess up his hair.

"Not the hair." Thorwald wiggled and pushed away from Burkhart before smoothing his hands over his blond hair. "Dude, really. Grow up."

"Thorwald, I'm going to kill you!" Niels, the youngest of the Rocchi children, ran into the garage, eyes furious. "What the hell is wrong with you?"

Leo covered his mouth to hold back the laughter. His omega brother's hair was baby poop green.

Burkhart whined but kept his lips pressed together.

Leo's sister Rosemarie was the last into the garage. She ran an eye over Niels's hair and shoved Thorwald. "Dye in the shampoo? Good one."

Leo and Burkhart's eyes met and neither of them could hold it in any longer. Laughter filled the garage.

"I hate you all." Niels stomped his feet. "I'm going to get Sonny to turn your heads into pecan pies. Let's hear you laugh then."

~

FOUR HOURS LATER, LEO AND HIS FAMILY GATHERED around a table and ate lasagna in the breakroom. Ravenpaw's considerable bulk stretched along the middle of the table, and the black cat happily nibbled on his treats.

"Sonny's food always makes me feel good," Rosemarie said before taking another bite.

"Me too," Leo's mom, Katrin, agreed. "Speaking of Sonny, did you send the reminder e-mail, Coleen?"

"Of course. I even remembered to send it to the Blackwoods and the other witch families we know." Coleen gave them a smug look and slid Ravenpaw a bit of sausage. "I got a reply from *the* Blackwood."

"Huh?" Thorwald eyed her. "There's only one?"

"No, you nitwit." Coleen leaned forward, eyes bright. "The head of the Blackwood family. He lives in Haverdell and is one of the senior members of the Witches Council."

"Really?" Leo almost missed his mouth with his fork. "Is he sending someone?"

Coleen shook her head and leaned back. "He has business to handle near here, so *he's* coming to celebrate Litha with us. He even offered to do the scrying for Sonny, but I told him that Sonny would probably want Myrtle to do it. He was super nice."

"I'm glad he's not a dickhead like some of the other witches," Katrin said. "Our Sonny deserves to be accepted as he is."

"Well, the man's from Haverdell, so he's used to seeing different species mating and marrying one another," Burkhart said, fixing a second plate of lasagna. "Thorwald and I will try to keep the rest of the family in line, but you know how they get when it's a celebration."

"This Litha celebration is going to be the best surprise." Coleen clapped excitedly. "Myrtle will do the Litha scrying for the baby and the protection blessing for Sonny, all his friends and family will be there, and, of course, we'll have a bonfire and dancing."

"Grandma invited Maddel and the rest of the neighbors," Rosemarie whispered. "Who wants to be the one to break it to Sonny that gnomes are coming to the Litha celebration?"

"Not it," Leo said, standing quickly and running to the door with his lasagna. "Not it, not it, not it."

~

THAT EVENING, LEO PARKED HIS TRUCK AT THE apartment complex, then got the empty lasagna pan from the passenger seat and let Ravenpaw out of his travel carrier. "Come on, Rav. Let's get inside and out of this damn heat."

"Meow." Ravenpaw hopped out of the truck and started for the stairs.

Leo took a moment to pick some of the Blackwood roses from the bush planted next to the door of their apartment building. It had become an evening ritual.

"Flowers for my sunshine," he whispered, smiling softly.

He ran up the stairs and found Ravenpaw waiting for him in front of their apartment. "I'm coming. I'm coming."

A wreath of Hawthorne wood and summer flowers decorated the door. Leo recognized a few of the flowers and remembered what Sonny had told him. "Lavender for love, geranium for protection, larkspur for laughter, and marigolds for happiness."

He opened the door and let Ravenpaw in first, before entering and closing and locking the door behind him.

Sonny was asleep on the couch, curled around Flufflepuff. A plate with the remnants of carrot cake sat on the table.

Leo bent and kissed Sonny's head before tucking a throw around him. He grabbed his phone and ordered delivery from the Indian restaurant down the road.

Sonny would likely wake up hungry, and he seemed to always want either strawberries or chicken curry.

When the order was placed, Leo sat on the edge of the couch and lightly ran his hand over Sonny's abdomen. Soon, Sonny's body would begin to more noticeably change, but Leo could already see tiny changes in his mate.

I hope Sonny likes the surprise, he thought absently. His mate deserved Leo's absolute best, and he swore he would always give it to him.

CHAPTER 27

*S*onny sipped his tea and fought back a yawn. "Why do we need to leave so early?"

Leo looked up from where he was packing the last of Flufflepuff and Ravenpaw's toys. "Grandma really wants to see you."

Sonny hummed happily and shook the bangles on his wrists. Janine had sent them to him last week. "I love her."

Leo leaned in and kissed his cheek. "She loves you too. Now, get a move on, sunshine."

Sonny looked around, eyes narrowed. "I don't see the honey cakes I made last night. Really, Leo? Those were for the trip. Now what are you going to snack on while you drive?"

Leo winced. "They looked so good, and I hadn't had breakfast yet."

Sonny fought back a smile and opened a cabinet. "You're lucky I made extras."

Leo's face brightened. "Yes! You're the best mate ever."

"You bet your sweet, bitable ass I am." Sonny grabbed more of his tea mixture while he was thinking about it. "I wish Aaron, Gemma, and Wendy were coming with us. I don't know why they needed to go to the beach this exact weekend. They didn't even say goodbye. Everyone is too busy to celebrate Litha, and it's not fair."

Sonny tried not to scowl. He really didn't mind spending the holiday with Leo and his grandparents, but he'd gotten a little spoiled over the past year. Everyone in the family loved get-togethers and celebrations, but no one could join them at the farm.

Leo pulled him into a hug, his warm hand soothing against Sonny's back. "Don't think too hard on it, sunshine. I'll carry our bags down to the car."

Sonny picked up the extra-large cat carrier. Ravenpaw and Flufflepuff liked riding together when possible.

Leo dropped the bags he had just picked up and rushed over. "I'll get that, love. Don't worry about carrying anything to the truck."

Sonny eyed him. "When did I become a delicate flower? I can carry the damn cat carrier."

Leo gave him a nervous look and picked his bags back up. "If you're sure."

Sonny rolled his eyes. "I love you, honey bear, even when you're way too protective."

"You wanted to go get a few herbs from your

rooftop garden, right?" Leo asked, giving Sonny an innocent look.

Sonny shook his head. "You're up to something, but I *do* want to bring some of our lavender to make Janine a wreath, so I'll go along with it. This time."

"Take your time," Leo huffed as he picked up Sonny's shoe bag. "Do you really need this many shoes for a weekend?"

Sonny looked over his shoulder as he walked to the door. "Don't you like my shoes, honey bear?"

Leo's eyes heated as he looked over Sonny's floral ankle strap flats, and his long, bare legs which were on display in his short, blue jean cutoffs. "I love your shoes. Maybe we don't have to get there so early."

Sonny giggled and ran out the door. "Focus, Leo."

Eventually, they managed to load the truck and buckle in. Sonny happily cuddled against Leo's side. He hugged Leo's arm as the city faded and they entered the suburbs. Nervousness settled in his stomach.

Do it now, Sonny. "Do you know why Litha is a special holiday."

Leo's nose scrunched up as he thought hard. "It's Summer Solstice and the longest day in the year. After Litha, each day grows shorter and shorter until Winter Solstice. It's a time of abundance. Right?"

Sonny smiled against Leo's arm. His bear was a good listener. "Yep. The God and Goddess are happily married and looking toward the future. It's a chance to let go of your past and plan for the year ahead. Time to take another step forward in life."

"We had fun last year." Leo grinned and tapped the steering wheel. "Lots of food and dancing."

"Don't forget the blessings of protection," Sonny added. "They're strongest when made on Litha."

"Meow." Flufflepuff's paw poked out of the carrier as his familiar reminded him of the topic at hand.

Sonny took a big breath and let it out. "It's also a special time for those who are pregnant."

Leo gave him a half smile. "How so? No one in our group was pregnant this time last year."

Sonny buried his face against Leo's arm for a moment, then peeked up. "A Litha scrying can tell expecting parents a lot about what the future will hold. It's also a perfect time for an early blessing on the baby."

"Really?" Leo's voice went high at the end of the word. "Well, do we know anyone that's pregnant?"

Sonny puffed his cheeks out. "Maybe."

"Maybe?"

"Remember when you said you wanted children?" Sonny asked, leaning his head on Leo's shoulder. "At our handfasting. In April."

Leo chuckled. "Yes, I do. I also remember all the fertility blessings people gave us. I also remember the green fertility candles you set up that night and every night until a couple of weeks ago. Then there's the fertility blessed strawberries and carrot cake you've been eating since our handfasting. Plus, I don't know if you know this, sunshine, but bear shifters have a keen sense of smell and can tell when their mate's scent changes with pregnancy."

Sonny growled and bit Leo's arm. "Are you telling me you know I'm pregnant?"

Leo laughed and leaned over to give Sonny a quick kiss, eyes staying on the road. "I'm saying everyone knows you're pregnant. It's been hard keeping Mom and Coleen from starting on a nursery in one of the guest rooms. Burk, Thor, and Dad have all been fighting the urge to bring you food, and Niels and Rosemarie have already started buying baby clothes. There was no stopping that."

Sonny scowled. "I haven't even told Myrtle and Aaron yet."

Leo eyed him before focusing on the road.

Sonny narrowed his eyes. "They already know too."

"Maybe."

Sonny leaned back in his seat, fighting a pout. "And they still couldn't spend Litha with us?" He groaned. "I'm being a selfish jerk, aren't I? People have their own lives and don't have to arrange everything just for me."

Leo grunted but took one of Sonny's hands and squeezed it. "How do you feel about the baby?"

Sonny hid his face and hugged Leo's arm again. "I'm so excited to expand our family, honey bear. We're going to have a bear shifter or a witch, but it doesn't even matter. We're going to love them no matter what. I already have the perfect name too."

Leo's grin was big and goofy. Sonny didn't even have to ask how his mate felt about the baby. It was written all over his face. "What name?"

"Rowan Aaron Rocchi. I'd make Aaron the first

234

name, but then we'd have two Aarons and that would be confusing."

"I like it," Leo said, still grinning.

"Are you nervous at all?" Sonny asked, fighting the butterflies dancing around in his gut.

Leo swallowed hard. "Hell, yeah. Honestly, I'm terrified. It's easy to say *I'll just love my kid and everything will be okay*, but what if I really do fuck up somehow?"

"I'm scared too," Sonny whispered. "A baby is a really big deal. We both have a lot of obligations. I love Miles and don't want to give up my apprentice, but I remember how much time Mother and Father spent with their apprentices instead of me. I don't want that for our child."

"We'll figure it out," Leo said, voice calm and steady. "You're aren't alone in this. Together, we'll teach them all about our traditions, both shifter and witch." He squeezed Sonny's hand again. "Tell me about your favorite Litha."

Sonny thought for a moment, then smiled. "I was about eight years old. Mom and Dad took their older apprentices to Haverdell to celebrate Litha with the Blackwood family, but I was grounded because they had found another of my stashes of skirts and jewelry. Anyway, I was staying with Myrtle while they were gone. She usually goes to the coast to spend Litha with Hester but had stayed in the city so I wouldn't be alone."

Leo's growl reverberated through the truck, and Ravenpaw and Flufflepuff started growling too.

"Settle down, you three," Sonny ordered with a laugh. "It gets better, I promise. So, Myrtle took me to a big celebration in one of the city parks. There was a bonfire and plenty of food and dancing. I was having so much fun, but Myrtle asked me if I wanted to see something special. She led me deeper into the trees and we found a fairy ring of white mushrooms."

Leo gave him a surprised look. "Really? Us kids always looked for those during our summers at the farm, but we've never seen any."

"They're usually rare, but if you look closely, you can find them on Litha. Myrtle said the Summer Solstice was a special time for fairies and other Fae folk."

"I always wanted to meet one of the Fae," Leo mused. "I saw a fairy once. She was a cute little bit, and Niels went to school with one of the Fae. He said the man was a bit standoffish."

Sonny shrugged. "I think they're just more comfortable in their own kingdom. Myrtle said there's a colony that lives in Haverdell, but that's the only one she knows about. Of course, fairies live all over, but they don't like cities, so I never see any."

Leo gave him a wry look. "I interrupted your story. Sorry."

Sonny laughed. "I almost forgot. So, Myrtle showed me the fairy ring, then she took out a bag of sugary treats and set them around the ring. A few moments later, fairies started pouring from the ring. They were so beautiful and colorful with their gorgeous little wings. They went right for the candy and devoured it."

"Wow," Leo whispered. "How many did you see?"

"Over thirty before I lost count." Sonny closed his eyes, and he could picture them all perfectly. "When they finished the candy, they flew to Myrtle and me. They were curious, so they played in our hair and clothes. They danced around us like butterflies, so Myrtle and I stood and danced too. We laughed so hard, and the fairies laughed too. It was the best Litha I've ever had."

"That sounds…" Leo's voice trailed off. "I want that for our kids. I want us to take them to the farm for Litha, and I want them to meet fairies and dance with them."

Sonny swallowed the lump in his throat. "I want that too." He patted Fluff's paw when it poked out of the carrier again. "You and me, we're going to be good parents. We have your parents and grandparents for good examples, and my parents and grandparents for bad examples."

"We have Myrtle too," Leo whispered. "I'm glad you were assigned to her when you were a kid."

"I don't know where I'd be without her." Sonny watched the suburbs fade into farmland and thick forests. "We'll love our baby, honey bear. The rest we can figure out, but that's the most important thing."

Leo kissed the top of his head. "As long as I have you with me, I'm happy."

The rest of the drive went quickly. Sonny had been to Leo's grandparents' home several times now, but he could never quite get used to the wildness of the area. *I'm definitely a city witch.*

When they pulled into Janine and Ronald's long driveway, Sonny sat up straighter and looked around. "Why are there vehicles lining the driveway? It looks busier than Christmas time. Wait. Is that Aaron and Gemma's car?" He turned to look at Leo, excitement building. "What's going on?"

Leo put the truck in park and turned to give him a smug look. "Did you really think our friends and family wouldn't be here for our baby's Litha scrying? Myrtle even brought her sister Hester."

Sonny jumped when people started pouring out of the large farm house. He grinned as he recognized all the Rocchi family members as well as his own friends. Devin and Tilisha waved from where they sat with one of Leo's lion shifter friends.

Burkhart opened the passenger side door and took the cat carrier. "There's my two favorite sweethearts."

"He's talking to the cats, isn't he?" Sonny asked wryly.

Leo snorted. "Need you ask?"

Rosemarie filled the open space when Burkhart backed up. Leo's sister grinned and pulled Sonny out of the car and into her arms. "I'm going to be the best aunt this baby ever had. That's the truth right there."

Sonny laughed when she scooped him up and carried him toward the house. "I can walk, Rose. Sheesh."

Janine's weathered face lit up when she saw him. "Oh, Sonny. I'm so happy for you and Leo. Wait until you see what I have for the baby."

"Love you, Grandma," he called out as Rosemarie carried him into the house.

He heard Myrtle's cackle before he saw her. His mentor and her sister, Hester, had Aaron and Gemma between them at the kitchen table. Several of Leo's aunts, uncles, and cousins sat around it and watched as the witches instructed them on making Litha wreathes.

Aaron held his daughter, Wendy, in his lap and grinned at Sonny. He wiggled his nose, making Sonny smile. When Wendy did the same thing, Sonny couldn't help but laugh.

"Use the citrine and jasper in your charm, Oscar," Myrtle said, pointing to a wreath Leo's uncle was making. "That will help your cattle production for the year if you hang it in your barn."

A second later, his mentor looked up and saw him. Her smile stretched wide and she winked.

How could I have doubted her? How could I have doubted any of them? Sonny's eyes watered, and he quickly wiped them on Rosemarie's shoulder. *This is how Litha is supposed to be.*

CHAPTER 28

The next morning, Leo woke up slowly, frowning as he patted Sonny's empty spot. Ravenpaw slept on Sonny's pillow, but Leo's mate and Flufflepuff weren't where they were supposed to be.

Leo grumbled as he sat up. "Ravenpaw, where did those two go?"

Ravenpaw opened one eye, stared at him a moment, then closed it.

Leo sniffed. "I see how it is."

The door slammed open as he was buttoning his pants. Burkhart stomped into the room, expression furious. "We have a problem."

Leo froze. "Sonny?"

Thorwald pushed in behind Burkhart. "He's fine. Grandma took him and Aaron for a walk in the woods."

Leo let the tension drain from his shoulders. "Thank the Goddess. What the fuck, Burkhart? You almost gave me a heart attack."

"Sonny's parents are here." Burkhart snarled. "They brought a few witches with them and are saying things that make me want to tear their heads off."

Leo growled. "Thorwald, please go make sure Sonny stays in the woods. I'm going to kick some ass."

Thorwald nodded and spun around, running from the room.

Burkhart threw Leo a shirt and followed him from the house, Ravenpaw stalking behind them.

A crowd of people were gathered in front of the farm house. Leo recognized Cynthia Thornton, Sonny's mom. The man beside her had Sonny's chin. *Travis, Sonny's dad.*

"We demand to speak with Somerset," Cynthia said, shoulders back and nose in the air. "This disgusting display of insolence has gone too far. It's one thing to mate a shifter, but another to bring abominations into this world. We won't let it happen."

Several witches stood behind her, arms crossed and faces hard.

The group of Rocchi bears and their friends teemed with agitation, snarls and growls breaking free. Rosemarie's mate, Kate, held a very angry rabbit shifter in her arms. Gemma wiggled, trying to get down to attack the witches, though Leo wasn't sure what she thought she could do.

This is going to be bad, Leo thought, even as he fought his own anger.

"I told you they were pieces of shit, didn't I, Hester?" Myrtle said, cracking her knuckles. "I'm going to enjoy this, Cynthia."

Hester grinned, wrinkled face full of joy. "I haven't been in a good fight in a while. This should be fun."

Travis cleared his throat. "Somerset cannot have these children."

These children? Leo frowned. Could the man see far enough into their future to see all of his and Sonny's kids?

"We have representation from the Witches Council with us, Myrtle. You and your sister shouldn't interfere." Travis glared at all the others. "None of you should interfere. This is a family matter."

"Family?" Jesse asked, voice hard. Katrin and he moved forward, hands already shifting into paws. "You come to our home and call my grandchild an abomination and dare order us around? You aren't Sonny's family. We are."

A few of Leo's family members shifted to their bear forms and moved forward to stand with Jesse and Katrin. Leo barely fought back his own shift. *Need a voice to solve this*, he told his bear.

"We have the Witches Council's approval," Travis said again, voice cracking as he backed up. "I did the scrying and have seen the little beasts. They aren't even witches."

Fuck being sensible. Leo growled and pushed to the front of the crowd, Burkhart behind him. "This is your last chance to get the fuck out of here. Litha scryings are sacred. Even I know that. That you did one without our permission is against the rules. Isn't it, Myrtle?"

"Yep," Myrtle said, a wicked smile on her face. "I'm

the only one they've given permission to, dick breath. You fucked up."

"Our rules are none of your concern, bear," Travis said, eyes narrowing.

The ground rumbled beneath the two groups, and Leo fought to keep his footing, his heart beating fast. *Earthquake? Here?*

A deep voice boomed from behind Leo. "Enough."

Leo turned. His grandpa and another man threaded through the crowd of bears. The man with Ronald looked ancient, but Leo could feel the power coming from him.

"Councilmen Blackwood," Travis said, mouth hanging open. "What are you doing here?"

The older man frowned and held up the bottle of beer he carried. "I came to celebrate young Somerset and his mate's first child. I was invited here for the scrying. I certainly don't recall the Council giving you any sort of support in harassing your son. In fact, we were rather disgusted by your bigotry." He stared at one of the men beside Travis. "You work for Councilman Winters, don't you?"

The man gave Blackwood a tentative nod. "My mentor is offering his personal support to Thorton and his wife. I've been ordered to see that Somerset Thorton doesn't give birth after mating a beast."

More of Leo's relatives shifted. Burkhart's hands on his shoulders steadied Leo enough to not shift and maul the disgusting man threatening his mate.

"As different as each species is, we are one people," Blackwood said, eyes hard. "You dare to impose your own ignorant bigotry on a young witch you've callously disowned? Over my smoldering corpse."

Movement at the edge of the woods caught his eye, and Leo turned when someone screamed his name. Sonny and Thorwald came from the woods at a run.

Sonny raced toward him, standing out in his rainbow-colored tennis shoes, denim overall shorts, and bright t-shirt. A baby rabbit shifter rode in the front pocket of the overalls. Aaron's daughter looked completely unconcerned about whatever was terrifying Sonny.

Sonny almost tripped but caught himself, making Leo growl. "Leo, save us!"

His nerves on edge, Leo shifted, his clothes shredding around him as he roared and ran to his mate.

Sonny threw an arm around Leo's neck and buried his face in Leo's fur. "Janine brought us to a fucking gnome village, Leo. There were thousands of them. We're lucky we escaped with our lives."

"I didn't know he could run that fast." Thorwald sounded shocked. He stood panting behind Sonny. "I'm sorry, Leo. I tried to keep him away."

More people came from the wooded walking path —Janine, Aaron, and several gnomes, and they didn't exactly look like they were about to murder one another.

"You were right, Janine. The poor dear is petrified," a familiar gnome said.

Leo waved a paw at Maddel. The older gnome was a nice woman who happened to be one of his grandma's best friends. She was only about six inches tall and walked beside Flufflepuff, hand stroking along the cat's side.

"There weren't thousands of gnomes, Sonny," Aaron said, face red from laughing as he stumbled behind Janine. "There were like forty or something. They tried to give you a cake."

Hmm, cake?

Sonny glared at him. "You're thinking about that cake, aren't you?"

Leo shook his head.

Wendy wiggled her nose and reached out to sniff Leo's ear.

Maddel patted Sonny's shoe. "Don't worry, sweetheart. You'll get to know us and see that we're not bad at all."

"Unhand my Sonny, gnome." Myrtle stomped over.

Hester chuckled as she followed her sister. "Please tell me you're not still mad about that gnome that kicked your ass when you were six. You deserved it, Myrtle."

"Gnomes are more dangerous than they look," Myrtle said, scowling. She pulled Sonny into her arms. "Who is she?"

Maddel nodded and introduced herself. "I see we'll need more than cake here."

Leo nuzzled Sonny's face and his mate sighed. "No, Maddel. I'm sorry I ran screaming. I should know that Janine wouldn't be friends with a murderous monster."

Myrtle snorted. "How much do we really know about Janine?"

245

Leo's grandma frowned and waved toward the two groups. "Why does it look like there's about to be a war on my front lawn?"

Sonny finally seemed to notice his parents, and the color drained from his face. "What are they doing here?"

Myrtle turned Sonny and pushed him into Janine's arms. "You hold him a moment. I have some witches to hex."

Leo growled and walked beside her as the two groups faced off.

Blackwood watched him with a smile. "Your love for you mate is obvious, Leo. Thank you for letting me attend this scrying." He turned to the gathered witches. "Now, I would like to get back to my beer, and Ronald here challenged me to a game of checkers. We don't have time for party crashers." He held his hands out to Myrtle and Hester. "Would you two lovely witches help me?"

Hester took one of his hands and Myrtle the other. The three witches closed their eyes, and Leo's fur stood on end as Blackwood's powerful aura grew stronger. He couldn't see the magic surrounding the three witches, but he could feel it.

He could also see the results.

The earth beneath Sonny's parents and their allies rumbled and moved, reshaping into a large hand. Cynthia and a few of the others screamed as they fell down, but Travis and many of the others tossed spells toward the earthen hand, though it did no good.

The hand picked the witches up and closed into a

fist before moving and cutting a path across his grandparents' yard, dirt churning beneath it. *Grandma isn't going to like that.*

When it reached the very edge of the driveway, the fist stopped and the dirt shifted again, changing into a hardened earth box with breathing holes.

Leo could barely hear the witches inside, screaming and tossing spells toward their prison.

Blackwood's eyes opened. "There. That will keep them in place until the proper authorities arrive to take them away. At the very least, they were trespassing, but we heard Travis and Cynthia's threats."

Myrtle scowled and let go of his hand. "Should have turned the fuckers into crickets and let the chickens have them."

Hester's eyes narrowed. "Agreed."

Blackwood gave the two sisters an amused look. "Sometimes, making a public example of them does more good. Do you think Somerset and his bear are the only interspecies mates that need the public support of the Witches Council?"

Sonny and the others approached, and Leo huffed out a laugh when he noticed Maddel was riding Ravenpaw. He hadn't even noticed their cat going to Sonny.

Sonny's eyes were sad as he watched the earthen box. "What did they say?"

Leo shifted, unconcerned with his nudity, and pulled Sonny into his arms. "Does it matter? Remember what you told me about Litha? It's a time to let the past go and look toward the future. Those people aren't your parents. Myrtle is. They aren't your family. We are." He gave Sonny a gentle kiss. "Let's forget those assholes exist and get to our celebration."

Sonny gave him a slow smile. "That's a good idea." He looked over his shoulder. "Let go of the past, Myrtle. Gnomes aren't so bad. That cake looked really good."

Myrtle scowled. "Don't sass me, *Somerset*. You being pregnant doesn't mean I can't turn your skin purple and your hair orange."

Sonny gave her a horrified look. "I wouldn't match at all."

The old witch smiled smugly. "Exactly."

CHAPTER 29

Sonny was a bit tired after his morning run for his life. He leaned back against a tree and watched as Thorwald and some of the Rocchi cousins got the bonfire going. The bear shifters joked as they tossed wood in, bodies already loose limbed from the beer they'd been drinking. Fortunately, Niels was there to supervise so no one ended up in the fire.

Tilisha and her family worked with some of the other guests to hang strings of summer flowers from the low branches of the trees in the clearing they had chosen for the celebration. *Mugwort for divination, wisteria for harmony and peace, and verbena to bring us closer to the God and Goddess.*

Ravenpaw was a short distance away, playing with the gnomes. Sonny had been shocked to find out that gnomes were very good with animals. They had fallen in love with Ravenpaw and Flufflepuff and were currently making flower crowns for his cats. *Gnomes really aren't that bad*, he thought, fighting the wiggle of doubt that filled his mind. *Janine trusts them.*

Gemma was still in her rabbit form. She hadn't moved from Sonny's side all morning, which made him think his parents' threats had been particularly nasty.

She curled against him, head pressed to his abdomen. Wendy sprawled over her with her chubby bunny butt pointed toward the sky.

Aaron bumped his shoulder. "Look at your bear, Sonny."

Sonny turned his head and watched Leo as he helped Myrtle and Hester decorate the altar they would use for the scrying and blessing. *My honey bear learned his flowers*, he thought with a smile.

Flufflepuff stretched across his shoulders as Leo placed the handful of mistletoe and St. John's wort they had picked beside the circle of amber stones. *Mistletoe for divination and health, St. John's wort for protection from those who would harm us, and amber to heal that which is broken.*

He rubbed his chest, hating that his parents still had the ability to hurt him.

Aaron took his hand and laced their fingers together. "Remember when you were afraid to talk to Leo when you two first met? You thought he would hate you."

Sonny gave his friend an irritated look. "Do you have to remind me of that now?"

Aaron watched him with wide blue eyes. "You thought he could never accept your genderfluidity because your parents didn't. They've fucked with your head long enough, Sonny. Over this past year, I've watched Leo grow to accept himself. He's pushed himself to learn about witch culture so he can love you as you deserve. He's pulled you into his family, and they've made you their own."

Sonny's heartbeat quickened. "He's my honey bear and the best mate in the world."

Aaron nodded. "I've also seen you become more *you*. You do more than accept Leo and his family; you always try to make life better for them. You've become one of them, and while you were taking care of them, something happened. Before, you would hide yourself away as much as possible. The only places you felt safe were at home or in the shop. Now, you're just *you* everywhere you go, and it's so beautiful, Sonny. You're beautiful."

Sonny closed his eyes, trapping his tears away. "I am beautiful. No matter what I wear, no matter what gender I'm feeling or not feeling today. I'm a beautiful person. We all are." He squeezed Aaron's hand. "I have an amazing family and the best brother in the world." Gemma rubbed her head against his abdomen, making him laugh. "The best sister too."

He watched as his mate looked up and smiled at him. Leo always smiled at him. He always looked at Sonny as if he was everything important in life.

"I think," he said, voice soft, "that life is about loving. Loving our mates, families, and friends, of course, but also loving the world around us and everything in it. I can't hate my parents. I want to, and they deserve it, but I don't want that weight on me.

They don't love me and it haunts them. Everything I do that they don't approve of eats at them and pulls them down. That's what they choose to carry. I'm choosing love."

"They really don't deserve it," Aaron said, growling.

Sonny shrugged. "I'm not forgiving them what they've done, but I'm choosing to let them go. They can sink under all that hate of theirs. That's their decision. Me? I'm going to focus on loving me and mine. That's what I want in my head and heart."

Leo said something to Myrtle, making her laugh, then turned and walked toward them. *He's so easy to love.*

Leo grinned and knelt in front of him. "Myrtle says they're ready, sunshine. Do you want to do the blessing or the scrying first?"

"Blessing," he said quickly, catching Flufflepuff when she jumped into his arms. "The scrying is for fun, but the blessing is the most important part."

Leo nudged Gemma and Wendy off Sonny's lap and helped him stand.

Aaron gathered his wife and daughter in his arms, laughing when they both refused to shift to their human forms. "You two are going full bunny, huh? I guess there are worse ways to enjoy a party."

An hour later, all their guests gathered around the altar. Miles and his parents were nearby, and Ravenpaw and Flufflepuff were curled up with Cookie and some of the other familiars.

Myrtle looked around them. "Any who wish to join in for a Litha blessing and baby scrying, come on up."

Sonny looked around hopefully. There were a lot of people here today, so surely someone else was pregnant too.

Rosemarie and Kate stepped forward, hand in hand. "We'll take that baby scrying and the blessing, please," Rosemaire said with a smile.

Sonny squealed and rushed to hug her. "Kate, you're pregnant?"

"Scent changed yesterday," Kate said, cheeks flushing.

Jesse and Katrin joined in the hug and soon all the Rocchi family was congratulating the young couple.

After six more people came forward, they all settled down around the altar. Leo and Sonny held hands as they knelt on one side while Myrtle sat on the other with her rune bag in her lap. Hester and Blackwood sat on either side of her, offering their strength for the rituals.

They all joined hands and Myrtle gave Sonny a wink before putting on her serious face. "The wheel of life turns and we find ourselves in the day of light and fire. Blessed be this Midsummer Solstice. The sun is at its peak, and the Goddess is heavy with child. Today we celebrate the light, for tomorrow that light will wane. Today we acknowledge the end of the waxing year and the beginning of the waning time. We say goodbye to the time of growth and fertility and welcome the seasons of harvest and wisdom. We say goodbye to a past of burdens and welcome a future of our own making."

They held their hands up high, and Myrtle closed

her eyes. Sonny's mind centered on the ring of amber on the altar. *Shield of protection and the healer of that which is broken.*

"On this day of longest light, we call forth the protection of the Goddess to see us through the waning time of darkness and introspection. Shield us from harm in the body, mind, and soul. Shield us from past cares and worries so that we might better shine for our Goddess." Myrtle opened her eyes. "Today, under the light of Litha, we call blessings of protection to all around us. We bless each of you by the earth, air, water, and fire that form the goddess."

As Myrtle's last word hung in the air, a soft yellow light surrounded her. Tendrils spread to Sonny and Leo, then to the others gathered around them. Sonny heard the gasps and excited chattering, but his focus was on the warmth filling him. Peace settled into him, and he felt tears prick his eyes. *Thank you, Goddess.*

Leo squeezed his hand and Sonny turned to him.

"Is this normal?" Leo whispered.

"Nope." Sonny grinned. "I think it's because Myrtle has Hester and Blackwood lending her strength. Now shut up and enjoy the blessing."

"Yes, dear." Leo kissed the back of his hand, then closed his eyes and smiled, soaking in the warmth from the light.

Several moments later, the warmth and the light faded, but the peace stayed inside him.

Myrtle opened her eyes and lowered their joined hands. "The Goddess is kind to gift us such a blessing." She let out a deep breath. "Okay, let's see what Sonny and his cat-bear have growing, huh? Then I want a look at Katie here."

The people around them cheered, and Sonny rolled his eyes. "Toss your runes, old woman."

Myrtle chuckled and held her rune bag to her lips. "First, the past guides us."

She closed her eyes and whispered an incantation. After a moment, she tossed the runes from the bag, watching them as they fell within the amber circle.

She considered them for a moment, then looked up. "The past has given you both strength of heart, though in different ways. Leo, your childhood has blessed you with an understanding of individual freedom and responsibility. Your children will benefit from your steadfast and hardworking nature." She smiled softly at Sonny. "Your childhood blessed you with an understanding of unconditional love. Your children will benefit from your generosity and purity."

Sonny blinked. "Purity? Me?"

Myrtle narrowed her eyes. "Don't question the Goddess, boy-o."

She gathered her runes and gently shook her bag before holding it to her lips again. Sonny fought a smile. He always thought she looked like she was tossing dice in Vegas when she did a scrying with her runes.

"The present molds us." The runes fell again and Myrtle looked them over. "You two are scared. You're in a place our ancestors have been for ages. New parents want the best for their child and fear taking the wrong step." She grinned. "You two aren't alone. Look around you."

Sonny squeezed Leo's hand and did as he was told.

Rosemarie gave him a rueful look. She completely got what Leo and he were filling, that was clear enough. Each of the others gathered around the altar felt the same fear he did.

Sonny let out a small breath and looked around the gathered crowd.

Leo's parents watched them with tears in their eyes. Aaron grinned and waved one of Wendy's little rabbit paws at him. Janine and Ronald watched him, eyes full of love. Everyone gathered around them was there to support them.

He met Leo's gaze, and they grinned at one another. Sonny suspected he may look as stupidly relieved as his mate did. "We can do this," he said.

Leo's grin widened. "Yeah. We have reinforcements."

"We're going to have a baby," Sonny whispered, letting it finally sink in. The pregnancy symptoms he had been feeling reminded him daily of his condition, especially at three in the fucking morning, but it was only now settling into him that it would all end with a tiny little being to hold and love.

"We are," Leo whispered back, eyes full of love. "Damn, I love you, sunshine."

"Love you too, honey bear."

"Keep your pants on, you two," Myrtle said and gathered the runes. "There's one more toss of the runes to see." She pressed the bag to her lips. "The future reveals our fate."

The runes fell into the amber circle, and Myrtle stared at them for several moments, eyes wide. Blackwood frowned and leaned over, eyes on the runes. Hester did the same and began chuckling.

"What?" Janine asked from the edge of the crowd. "What do you see about the baby?"

"You used a lot of fertility magic, didn't you?" Blackwood asked with a grin.

Sonny narrowed his eyes. "Don't judge me. I wanted a baby."

"You'll have three," Hester said, chuckling.

Sonny felt the blood drain from his face and leaned into Leo's side.

"Like, over the next ten years?" Leo asked, brow furrowed in confusion.

"Like, in about eight months," Hester said dryly. "Triplets, cat-bear."

"Oh, fuck," Leo whispered and hugged Sonny. "Oh, fuck."

"I don't know what dickwad thought he saw," Myrtle said quietly, "but I see two bear shifters and a little witch with a bear cub familiar."

Sonny gasped, the panic unfurling in his gut suddenly lessoning. He could see them clear as day in his heart's eye. "Rowan, Juniper, and Ash."

Leo's laugh was full of joy. "I see them, Sonny. Juniper has your eyes and chin. Rowan looks a lot like Burkhart and me, and Ash looks like Mom."

Sonny and Leo sat in a daze as Myrtle did the

scryings for the others gathered at the altar. He They focused enough to cheer when Myrtle revealed that Rosemarie and Kate would have healthy twin brown bear shifters, but that was about it.

Sonny leaned against his mate and watched their future unfold as the scrying mists lingered in his mind. He could see their little ones running through a meadow with their cousins, Juniper's bear cub running clumsily beside them.

It was a damn good life, but... "Shit, we're going to need a nanny."

CHAPTER 30

ONE YEAR LATER

*L*eo yawned, eyes barely staying open as he sat against one of the large oak trees in what had officially become the Litha clearing at his grandparents' farm. A large bonfire roared at the center and their family and friends gathered around, eating and laughing.

Thorwald and Burkhardt were leading the dancing, both in their bear forms of course. Jesse and Ronald were at the grill, doing their best to keep the chicken and steak platters full while Katrin, Neils, and Devon refilled bowls of vegetables and fruit dishes. Rosemarie and Kate were cuddled together a few trees over with their little ones, Samantha and Joy.

He looked around, but couldn't find Coleen. He growled then looked for Philip, but didn't see his friend either. Lately, he'd grown a bit suspicious of the way the lion shifter was watching Coleen. In high school, Philip had always had a crush on Leo's big sister, but had never tried anything.

"Fucker better not mess with my sister," he muttered, then winced and looked down.

Rowan slept curled in his lap, content to stay in his bear cub form for the day. The youngest of the triplets reminded Leo a lot of himself. He was a shy and sleepy bear. Fortunately, he was sleeping.

Ravenpaw looked up from his own nap. He slept curled around Rowan. Ravenpaw blinked once, yawned wide, then went back to sleep.

Lucky cat, he thought.

A familiar gurgling sounded from behind him, and he looked over his shoulder. Ash gurgled again as Leo's Uncle Oscar carried her through the woods in a baby sack. The man was in his bear form and held the top of the sack delicately between very sharp teeth.

There were several Rocchi bears shifted and playing in the trees, and they each took a turn carrying little Ash. The eldest of the triplets was a wild one, full of energy and joy in both her human and bear form. Leo dreaded the day she learned the walk.

Where's my Juni berry? He looked around for his little witch and spotted Myrtle with Juniper.

The old woman adored all the triplets, but called Juniper her *special bean*. She currently had the baby on her hip and walked around the clearing, chatting to Juni about the plants they saw.

He looked to his right when Gemma sat beside him. She held Wendy in her arms. The little girl was in her rabbit form again.

Gemma nodded toward their left. "What do you think that bunch is getting up to?"

Sonny, Aaron, and Miles were by the desert table, cackling together even though they were clearly trying to be quiet. They were replacing the plate of chocolate chip cookies with *something*. Flufflepuff supervised from a distance, eyes watching them carefully.

"I heard Sonny and Aaron talking about farting cookies last night," Leo said, yawning again. "I had baby duty though, so that could have been my imagination. I've seen a lot of things in the night."

Gemma chuckled and nodded at Wendy. "I've been there. Do you need Aaron and me to take a round again so you and Sonny can get some rest?"

Leo sighed. "We need something. Three babies are hard to handle in the middle of the night. We'll handle it, but we won't say no to help. Don't tell Sonny, but I talked to Dad about going to part-time at the garage. Myrtle loves watching the kids during the day, but she's retired and should be doing fun things like *yoga with rabbits* or something like that."

Gemma smacked his leg. "Me and her only did that once, so shut it. You better talk to Sonny first. He's hiring that new witch, so he'll have more time."

"Ludwig specializes in making spelled soaps and candles," Leo said, scratching Rowan's sides and back. "He'll be busy for a while filling inventory. I really don't mind working less hours. I love spending time with the trips anyway."

Wendy hopped from Gemma's lap and sniffed Rowan's nose for a moment before settling in for a snuggle with her favorite bear.

"I don't know." Gemma gave him a doubtful look. "I

still feel bad that Aaron waited to open his restaurant until last month so I didn't have to take time off from work to watch Wendy. He says he wouldn't have had it any other way, but that doesn't change how I feel."

Sonny, Aaron, and Miles snuck away from the table and headed their way. Sonny smiled wide as Leo watched him. His beautiful mate had told Leo that he was feeling "a little more neutral" today. He wore a pair of khaki shorts and a PRIDE t-shirt with his tan flat sandals and gold bangles.

Leo loved how Sonny was so in tune with himself. He didn't hesitate to express himself through his clothes and jewelry and grew less and less self-conscious with each day that passed.

Sonny knelt beside him and kissed him deeply, tasting of pure honey. Memories of their early morning loving heated Leo's blood, and he was reluctant to let Sonny end the kiss.

His mate gave him a knowing look. "Myrtle said she had a surprise for us and all the kids."

Leo frowned. "Do we really trust Myrtle?"

Sonny snorted, then stood up. "Come on, honey bear. I'll grab Ash."

"Good luck," Leo said wryly and stood up, Rowan, Wendy, and Ravenpaw in his arms. *They're getting heavier every day.*

Sonny chased after Oscar, laughing when Leo's uncle increased his pace. "Give me my baby, Uncle Oscar! We have surprises to see."

IT TOOK ALMOST AN HOUR, BUT SONNY HAD FINALLY convinced Oscar to come with them deeper into the woods. The bear still carried Ash, but now Miles rode on his back as well, Flufflepuff and Ravenpaw seated in front of him. Cookie followed along behind them.

Sonny curled into Leo's side, eyeing the trees in suspicion. "I still say these trees are watching us."

Leo rolled his eyes. "They're just trees. Calm down."

Sonny narrowed his eyes. *My honey bear better watch the sass.*

A tiny gnome peeked over a hollow in one of the oaks, starling him. "Hey, Sonny."

Sonny's heartbeat spiked for a moment before settling down. "Lala! I've been looking for you since we got here yesterday."

The teenager scooted out of the hollow and sat on the edge. Whereas most gnomes dressed in traditional gnome clothing and hats, Lala was embracing their gender fluidity and wore a mish mash of styles. Sonny adored them.

They had bonded last Christmas when Lala's parents introduced them.

When Lala came out to their parents, Hansel and Luelle had contacted Janine and set up a meeting between Sonny and Lala. They wanted their child to have as much support as possible and thought it might be nice for them to meet.

Lala let Sonny pick them up and set them on his shoulder. "Where were you?"

"I was helping set up Myrtle's surprise. I can't wait for you all to see. It's right ahead in the next clearing."

The comfortable weight of Leo's hand in his gave Sonny the feeling of safety he needed to appreciate the forest around him. "Okay, so what's this surprise?"

"You'll see," Lala said, voice smug.

Sonny gasped when he saw the large fairy ring. "I've never seen one that big."

"That's what Gemma said our first night together," Aaron said, smirking.

Sonny snickered.

Gemma snorted. "I was talking about your big toe."

Sonny smacked Gemma's arm. "Don't talk about Big Billy Joe that way. He's a mutant toe that's building his strength to save the world one day."

"Are you brats done?" Myrtle asked, brow raised. "I swear the triplets are better behaved than you lot and they drool all the time."

"So does Kate when she sees me naked," Rosemarie said from behind him, setting off everyone's laughter again.

Myrtle groaned. "I guess we don't *have* to see the fairies if you all would rather just joke around all day."

"No," Sonny said shaking his head. "Leo really needs to see them. Remember when I told you about them, honey bear?"

Leo smiled at him, eyes soft. "It's your favorite Litha memory."

"Well, it was until last Litha." Sonny leaned up and rubbed his nose against Leo's.

"Disgusting lovey nonsense," Thorwald said, huffing.

"You'll meet your mate soon enough," Myrtle said,

eyes narrowed on Leo's brother. "Where's Burkhardt and Neils?"

"Neils is flirting with Ludwig, and Burkhart was hitting the desert table," Thorwald answered, crossing his arms. "What's all this about fairies?"

"Take a seat, folks." Myrtle waited until Sonny was settled on the ground next to Leo, then handed him Juniper. "Hold my special bean while I get this done."

Sonny leaned into Leo. "Sometimes I think she might love the triplets more than her pot plants."

Leo looked doubtful. "I don't know. She really likes her special brownies."

Oscar gently set Ash down in front of them. Sonny unwrapped her and smiled when she shifted to her bear form.

"Thanks, Oscar." He settled Ash in his lap with Juniper, then patted the ground. "Come on, big guy. You need to see the fairies too."

The big brown bear lay down beside him, and Miles climbed off, bringing the cats with him. He snuggled into Oscar's side and pulled Cookie and the cats around him.

Sonny looked around. All of the children and several of the adults had gathered in the clearing. *They're going to love this.*

Myrtle stood in front of them. "Okay, settle down loud mouths. Litha is a special day for many reasons, but one of those is that it's a time when the barrier between here and Fae kingdom is almost non-existent. Many of the Fae and other species from their homeland use this time to travel back and forth."

She waved to the plates of sugary treats spread out in front of the circle. "Now fairies are particularly fond of sugar. If we're quiet and patient, we may just have some visitors."

"We can be quiet," Miles said, voice determined. "I really wanna see the fairies."

Myrtle gave him a fond look. "Good boy. Okay, sit and watch, folks."

Sonny settled his head on Leo's shoulder and enjoyed the moment of quiet. Ever since the triplets had been born, he and Leo hadn't gotten much sleep. Now that they were going on four months, it was getting a little better, but Sonny could still feel the pull of exhaustion.

His eyes closed for a moment, but Leo's gasp made Sonny sit up.

Fairies were flying out of the ring of mushrooms. Sonny studied them closely as they attacked the snacks.

The creatures looked so much like their Fae cousins, but were tiny in comparison. Their wings were a variety of colors and shapes. Some resembled butterflies while others looked more like dragonflies. They all wore traditional fairy clothes of leaves and flowers sewn together.

"They're beautiful," Leo whispered, eyes wide.

Sonny watched him for a moment. *They have nothing on you, honey bear*. His mate's open wonder was a lovely thing.

Sonny still found it hard to believe they'd been together for over two years now. Sonny loved him more with every day they spent together, and his heart still fluttered when he saw him for the first time each morning.

As the fairies finished the snacks, they looked around curiously, flying closer to the people gathered around. There were well over a hundred at that point.

"Oh goodness," Lala said, still sitting on Sonny's shoulder. "I've never seen so many."

One green-haired, dragonfly winged fairy settled on Rowan's head and giggled, voice tinkling as she pet him.

Others flitted around the children, seeming to delight in their laughter and awe.

Sonny smiled wide when a purple butterfly winged fairy landed on Leo's head and starting playing with his hair. The look on his mate's face looked an awful lot like Miles' did at that moment.

"What's that now?" Myrtle asked, frowning when the ring of mushrooms almost seemed to shiver.

Sonny watched as the ring expanded, spreading out another two feet. The grass in the middle danced in a breeze that Sonny couldn't feel. It shimmered, becoming a green and brown blur as a much larger figure rose from the ring.

"One of the Fae," Leo whispered, mouth falling open.

The young Fae flew high above the ring. He had light brown skin, curly black hair, and bright green eyes. His butterfly wings were a magnificent mix of green, yellow, and black, and his ears curved into sharp points. He carried more weight than was fashionable, but Sonny thought he looked absolutely beautiful. *Fuck fashionable*, he thought and hugged Ash and Juniper.

The Fae held a suitcase in one hand and a large orange cat in the other. Several fairies danced around him as he landed.

"Hi," the Fae said cheerfully. "I'm Leif." He looked around at all the children and babies, then focused on Leo and Sonny. "Mr. Blackwood wasn't lying. Those babies of yours are adorable."

Myrtle squinted up at Leif. "Blackwood sent you?"

Leif nodded, smiling brightly. "I'm a nanny. He hired me to help Somerset Rocchi and his mate with their triplets."

Sonny and Leo looked at one another for a moment, but Sonny knew they were of one mind on this. "Welcome to the family," Sonny said, smiling widely. "We'll set up a room for you at the apartment as soon as we get home."

Leif grinned again, green eyes shining. His wings fluttered. "Perfect! I'm so excited to see the city. I've never been out of Haverdell."

The bush to their right shuddered as something big moved through it.

Sonny squealed and climbed into Leo's lap, pulling Juniper and Ash with him. He maneuvered so he wasn't sitting on poor Wendy and Rowan.

Leo's arms wrapped around him and his bear rumbled with laughter. "It's just Burk."

Burkhart crashed into the clearing, eyes glaring as they landed on Sonny. A loud fart sounded around him and the clearing went silent. Even the fairies stopped to stare at the bear shifter.

"What the hell was in those cookies, Sonny?" Burkhardt scowled as another loud fart sounded. "I swear I'm not doing that. It's like farts are following me around."

Sonny collapsed in giggles against Leo's chest. He looked at Aaron and Miles. "The cookies are a success."

"Oh, that's just mean," Lala said, giggling.

Another loud fart sounded and that was all the crowd needed to start laughing. Even the fairies rolled in the air, shaking with laughter.

Burkhardt's face turned red and he started toward them, revenge in his eyes. Two steps in, he froze in place, eyes widening. The large man looked around as he sniffed the air.

Another fart sounded, but Burkhardt ignored the laughter and sniffed around the clearing until he came to Leif.

The Fae waved. "Hi. Do you need a gas pill? I have some in my bag."

Burkhardt ignored the next loud fart too and stared at Leif, eyes full of awe. "You're beautiful."

Leif blinked, cheeks flushing. He patted his tummy self-consciously. "You don't have to say that. I'll give you gas-x no matter what."

Sonny and Leo looked at each other, eyes wide. "Mates," they whispered at the same time.

AFTERWORD

Thank you for reading "Carrot Cake and a Witch's Surprise." This is book four in a series of short stories called Holiday Omegas, and concludes the story of Leo and Sonny. The next book in the series will begin Burkhardt and Leif's story. "Muddy Paws and a Fae's Wings," will be out in October, 2020.

ALSO BY C.W. GRAY

Charybdis Station Chronicles – science fiction/fantasy, mpreg

The Blue Solace Series

http://mybook.to/BlueSolaceSeries

1. The Mercenary's Mate
2. The General's Mate
3. The Soldier's Mate
4. The Lieutenant's Mate
5. The Engineer's Mate
6. The Captain's Mate
7. The Rebel's Mate

Charybdis Station

1. Death's Mate – *Coming Soon*
2. Fire's Mate – *Coming Soon*
3. Rune and Silas – *Coming Soon*

The Hobson Hills Omegas – non-shifter, mpreg, omegaverse

http://mybook.to/HHOseries

1. Falling for the Omega
2. Snow Kisses for My Omega
3. Romancing the Omega

4. Healing the Omega
5. A Pint for my Omega
6. Unraveling the Omega
7. The Alpha's Christmas Wish
8. Convincing the Alpha
9. Title TBA – Sheriff McKenzie's Book – *Coming Soon*

Hobson Hills Shorts – short stories from the world of Hobson Hills Omegas

1. The Beta's Love Song – http://mybook.to/BetaLoveSong
2. Bennett's Dream – http://mybook.to/BennettsDream
3. Justin's Journey – http://mybook.to/JustinJourney
4. Grey's Gift – http://mybook.to/GreyGift
5. Hobson Hills Shorts: Volume One – http://mybook.to/HHOShortsVolumeOne

Holiday Omegas Shorts – holiday short stories from the world of The Silver Isles – paranormal, mpreg, omegaverse

http://mybook.to/HolidayOmegaSeries

1. Cauldron Cake Pops and a Witch's Kiss
2. Sugar Cookies and a Witch's Love
3. Candy Hearts and a Witch's Ring
4. Carrot Cake and a Witch's Surprise
5. Muddy Paws and a Fae's Wings – *Coming in October 2020*

The Silver Isles – paranormal, mermen, mpreg, omegaverse

http://mybook.to/TheSilverIsles

1. The Guppy Prince
2. The Not so Little Merman
3. The Sea Witch – *Coming Soon*

Book 2.5 – "A Mate from the Deep"

http://mybook.to/AMateFromTheDeep

If you would like to keep up with releases, please like and follow me on Instagram (@c.w._gray) or Facebook (@cwgrayauthor), join C.W. Gray's Reading Nook on Facebook, or visit my website at https://cwgray-author.com